WINCHELL MINK

The Misadventure Begins

Steve Young

📖 HARPERCOLLINS*PUBLISHERS*

Library of Congress
Cataloging-in-Publication Data
Young, Steve, 1947–
Winchell Mink : the misadventure begins /
Steve Young.— 1st ed.
p. cm.
Summary: When a bullied eleven-year-old boy is
transformed into his pet turtle, he finds himself
catapulted on a series of bizarre adventures.
ISBN 0-06-053499-0 — ISBN 0-06-053500-8 (lib. bdg.)
[1. Adventures and adventurers—Fiction. 2. Turtles—
Fiction. 3. Bullies—Fiction. 4. Humorous stories.]
I. Title.
PZ7.Y883Wi 2004   2003021437
[Fic]—dc22

Typography by Amy Ryan
1 2 3 4 5 6 7 8 9 10

First Edition

To Matthew and everyone else
who has ever been told that they were different
and discovered that they couldn't have asked
for a better compliment

The catfish will walk,
The white wolf will fly,
Young braves become turtles,
Only gods know why.

—nineteenth-century Native American
Proverb made up by twenty-first-century
Los Angeles native

ONE

The Beginning of This Story

On this particular day, I did what I did at the end of every school day . . . run home. I would have much rather walked, but with the large number of bullies chasing me, I felt that running served me better.

"Yo, Dink, whataya afraid of!" yelled one massive bully.

I hated my name: Winchell Mink. It was too easy to rhyme. Mink. Fink. Dink. Pink. Stink. Mink the Tiddley-wink. I wanted a name that couldn't be made fun of. Say, like, *Orange*. Can't rhyme it and it's loaded with vitamin C.

"Yeah, Stink. 'Fraid you're gonna smell up the place?" belched an even larger bully.

My mother told me that Mink was a name to be admired;

that our family descended from the great fourteenth-century explorer Magellan "Whoops" Mink, the only voyager who actually fell off the edge of the Earth.

"Mink, Mink, the stupid Mink!" screamed a fast-approaching bully with limited rhyming skills. "We ain't gonna hurt you, Winchell . . . much."

To top it off, my parents had to stick me with *Winchell*. The fact that the second *l* was silent didn't make it any easier to take.

"Hey, Fink. Name three countries bordering Venezuela," quizzed the leader of the bullies, who had long before decided to become a geography teacher.

It would be bad enough if they were all just your run-of-the-mill bullies. But this bully bunch was led by the deadly clever Clayton Moore, the meanest and most articulate bully known to bullykind.

"Mink-a-dung, my good fellow. Are you hastening for asylum behind your *madre*'s apron?"

Hastening? Asylum? Madre? At least with most bullies, there's a pretty good chance that you are smarter than they are and in twenty or thirty years they'll probably end up in jail or serving burgers. With Clayton, becoming a dictator of a small country with weapons of mass destruction was more likely.

Clayton always had to make a big deal out of his being multilingual. The worst was when he made fun of me in Latin.

"Mihi placet quod huiusmodi ignavus es!" ("It pleases me that you are such a coward!")

Being put down never feels good, but having no idea what someone is saying to put you down is downright maddening.

Anyone who listened to Clayton would think that everything bad—homework, cafeteria food, adults not letting you stay out late, just to name a few—was all my fault. 'Cause I was a Mink. I know that sounds ridiculous, but some kids will believe anything.

"Yo, Minkster! Your momma wears dresses and sometimes an apron!"

You could always tell when they were running low on put-downs.

"Gotcha!" It's not like they needed to say much more once they caught me.

(Author's note: I've omitted the next scene due to the violent nature of my capture.)

Two
The Cliff ♪ ♩

When I reached home, the battle scars were obvious. With a head a bit too large for my body and ears a bit too large for my head, wounds above the neck were difficult to hide.

My mother was extremely concerned.

"Why do you and your friends have to play so rough? You're going to get blood all over the carpet."

I said she was *concerned,* not *sensitive.*

Here's when Clayton was most arrogant. While most bullies would take off as soon as a parent showed up, Clayton would stick around to drive home the final nail.

"Not to worry, Mrs. Mink. I was fortunate enough to be passing by when I came upon your Winchell dillydallying much too close to the edge of . . .

THE CLIFF♩♪♩."

"Winchell!" screeched Mom.

"As soon as I was cognizant of Winchell's loss of equilibrium," Clayton continued, "I was fortuitous enough to counteract his predicament by grasping his closest reachable limb and pulling him to safety."

My mom just stood there for a second, not saying a word. Even adults had a tough time trying to figure out what the heck Clayton was saying. But she had heard the word *cliff*. Boy, did she hear it.

"Winchell! You were playing near . . .

THE CLIFF♩♪♩?"

My parents had reminded me at least a zillion and a half times, "Don't go near . . .

THE CLIFF♩♪♩!"

If there was anything that worried Mom, it was that I might wander too close to the edge of the cliff and . . . you know. The *falling off, becoming dead* thing.

As much as I wanted to check it out, I knew that going anywhere near the cliff would be far too risky. My parents had promised if I fell off the cliff and smashed myself to smithereens . . . no more birthday gifts.

"I attempted to explain to the boy the ramifications of his actions, Mrs. Mink," Clayton slimed in, "but you know Winchell."

Of course she knew me. She was my mom. But Clayton always liked asking questions he knew the answers to.

"Mom. I didn't go near . . .

THE CLIFF ♪♩.

Clayton is a . . . a . . . big fat liar."

In fact, Clayton was far from a "*big fat* liar." Oh, he was a liar, for sure, but he was not only quite small, he was also in extremely good condition.

"Winchell. It's bad enough that you have to risk your own life, but to belittle this boy who actually saved you . . . I just don't know where you get your manners. Now wash up and go to your room," Mom snarled.

As I left, I caught a glimpse of my mom hugging Clayton. As luck would have it, Clayton was able to catch a glimpse of me glimpsing him. Clayton seized the moment.

"Don't you worry, Mrs. Mink. I'll keep an eye out for Winchell. I'm sure he'll soon grow out of this awkward stage."

Totally disgusted, I dragged myself up the stair (we were

so poor my parents could afford only one step) to my room.

My parents tried as hard as they could to provide a decent home, but as I said, we weren't rich. My dad always liked to say, "The Earth and the stars, what else do we need?" How about a floor and a roof? All we could manage were walls, and only three of those. Our house was a triangle.

We couldn't even afford any real furniture. We just used pictures of furniture that Mom would cut out of catalogs.

The walls of my room were papered with posters containing sayings my parents thought would inspire me. All they did was remind me of the many different ways my life didn't work.

THE TRUTH WILL SET YOU FREE.

YOU ARE SPECIAL.

KEEP YOUR PRIORITIES IN ORDER.

SLOW BUT STEADY WINS THE RACE.

WHEN THE STUDENT IS READY, THE TEACHER WILL APPEAR.

YOU CAN'T TELL A BOOK BY ITS COVER.

THERE'S NO PLACE LIKE HOME.

EXPERIENCE IS THE BEST TEACHER.

And of course, the ever-popular DO NOT READ THIS QUOTE.

At the time, I really didn't know what most of that stuff meant.

What garbage, I had thought. The only poster that made any sense to me was the one with the quote YOU TAKE THIS POSTER DOWN AND I SWEAR I WILL PUT MY TWO FINGERS IN YOUR NOSTRILS AND RIP YOUR NOSE OFF YOUR FACE.

Chirp-chirp-chirp.

Oh, yes. My babies. Right outside my window sat a nest full of hungry baby robins. Because of the little birdies' habit of falling out of the nest, their folks had abandoned them. My compassionate dad suggested—no way to put this gently—he wanted to flush them. He said it was the only humane thing to do. Boy, one day I'm going to need a lot of therapy.

I took the nest from the tree in the front of the house and hid it in the bush near my window. Like a good foster parent I fed the babies, diapered them, wiped their beaks whenever they ran. And, yeah, when it was time for them to go to sleep, I'd kiss 'em good-night. Not on the beaks. I mean, there are limits.

I didn't mind taking care of them, although the only way they would take the . . . um . . . worms was if I fed the worms to them from my mouth. To tell you the truth, with a little salt and ketchup, they weren't bad. Weren't good either.

After putting the birdies beddy-bye, it was time to feed my best friend, the not-very-human-at-all Hannibal. And herein lies my story.

skills. And her writing me a note was out of the question since she lacked an opposable thumb or decent pen. Since that time, Hannibal and I were inseparable, except for whenever I would leave my room without her.

After feeding her, and this is hard to admit, I lay in bed and cried. Everything seemed so dark. Of course much of this had to do with the fact that it was nighttime and I had my light off. I turned it on and still I was filled with hopelessness. At least something filled me. I had missed dinner.

THREE

Hannibal

Hannibal was my best friend. She was also a box turtle that I had found years ago when she tried to cross a four-lane highway.

She had been stuck in the middle of the road with cars whizzing by, just missing her. I darted into traffic and scooped up the confused yet determined turtle just before a large Mercedes sedan was about to smash her shell to smithereens.*

Unfortunately I had brought Hannibal back to the same side of the road where she had started her cross-highway venture, quite some time before. Hannibal didn't have the heart to tell me of my mistake. She also lacked the verbal

---

★ *SMITHEREENS* ARE ALSO KNOWN AS "TINY LITTLE SMITHERS."

FOUR

The Zillion and One Reasons I Hate School

As bad as today was, I knew that tomorrow wouldn't be any better. I would have to go to school, and all my troubles would begin again.

I wasn't too thrilled with the whole *getting an education* thing anyway. I figured that if I didn't know it by then, I would get along fine without it. Anyway, I had heard that "Experience is the best teacher." It had to be better than any of the teachers I had up till then. Especially Mrs. Kiddidle, my third-grade teacher with breath so bad, legend has it, it once stopped a runaway albino rhinoceros in its tracks.

Although I really tried to stay out of fights, I always found myself smack-dab in the middle of some scuffle. Or should

I say, "on the end." The *receiving* end. It seemed that a day did not go by without me getting beat up. To make matters worse, I felt that ratting out someone, even someone who beats you up for no reason, was about the worst thing a kid could do. So whenever a teacher or counselor showed up, I wouldn't turn in the real culprit. Unfortunately the real culprit would put all the blame on me. So I was considered a troublemaker and I regularly found myself being hauled down to the principal's office.

Recess was no better. In games on the playground, my lack of coordination made me the last one chosen for any game. That is, if I were chosen at all. Once, after spending two hours trying to get my baseball glove on, I realized we were playing football.

Sometimes, even when there were no sides to be chosen and there was absolutely no one else playing, some kid would put up a sign that said IF YOU READ THIS AND YOUR NAME IS WINCHELL MINK, YOU CANNOT PLAY.

I hate to admit this, but my attitude stunk big time. I hated my name. I hated the bullies, especially Clayton. I hated school. I hated my house. I hated my parents. I hated asparagus, the duck-billed platypus, and especially the spelling of the word *psychology*. What sane reason is there for starting that word with a *p*?

Everything was a battle, and right now it seemed like the whole world was against me . . . except for the people of Portugal, who always found time to send a postcard or two.

So it comes as no surprise that I regularly wished I were someone different. It was always, "I wish I was this . . . " or "I wish I was that . . . " Back then I never seemed to finish my sentences, but it was clear that I was unhappy. Especially that one night.

FIVE

I Wish I Were Dea . . .

As I lay in bed and thought over the events of the day, I had never felt so hopeless. In fact, hopeless was an understatement. I felt more than hopeless. I felt . . . hopelesser. And I hated being me. How I wished I could just choose to be someone else. Even Clayton. Boy, I was in bad shape.

That's when it hit me. My birthday was in two days. A time of celebration. But I had nothing to celebrate. As crummy as everything was, I had almost forgotten my birthday. Why even bother having a party? It's not like anyone would show up. And who wants to hear "happy birthday" when there's absolutely nothing happy about it?

Boy, was I a dud. The worst kind. I failed at everything I tried. How bad a failure was I? When I tried to fail, I was unsuccessful. I would actually fail at failure. I was sick of failing, and I never wanted to fail again.

I decided that I would never have another birthday and feel this way. I would do what any right-minded Mink would do in that situation—quit.

As I was about to fall asleep, the last words I uttered were more ominous than any I had ever uttered before.

"I wish I were dea . . . "

I had not finished my sentence, but the threatening intent of my incomplete thought was particularly . . . *threatening*.

Normally Hannibal would just let me grumble. But this time was different. This time the "I wish I were dea . . . " comment must have troubled Hannibal deeply.

I knew she wouldn't want me dea . . . What I didn't know then was that Hannibal had decided something had to change. Not just something. Everything. I had to go through a great metamorphosis (if I didn't want to sound so smart, I would've said *change* again). Hannibal knew it was time for me to truly experience life.

Oh, have I mentioned that Hannibal was not your typical box turtle? Well, she wasn't. She was, in fact, an enchanted turtle who had descended from the Great Mystical Turtles of the Tortoissaic Period, long since thought to be extinct.

The Mystical Turtles were able to communicate tele-pathically, although, due to their poor short-term memory, most of them had forgotten how to do it. Luckily Hannibal hadn't.

That evening, while I slept in my picture of a bed, Hannibal set about telepathically inputting the necessary data into my mind—data that would change my life forever. And this, ladies and gentlemen, boys and girls, this was not as easy as it may seem. Okay, communicating telepathically is not such a big deal, but you also have to translate turtle terminology into human kid vocabulary.

After doing her translating thing, Hannibal went to sleep, as she would need much rest for the adventure that awaited both of us.

There's more. Much more, but at this point, if I were you, I would head over to the next chapter, as I can assure you, you don't want to be here while we sleep. Hannibal snores much worse than your dad.

SIX

The Journey Begins

Early the next morning, while everyone in the house was asleep, I woke up. Something was clearly different. My first thought was not the usual, "Oh, man, I gotta go to school," or the way more important, "I really gotta go to the bathroom." Instead a voice in my head told me to go out and "experience life." It was a weird voice. You know, kind of what a turtle might sound like if it could talk.

An unmistakable feeling of energy and excitement filled every nook and cranny of my body. I've had my nook filled before, but never my cranny. It was quite eerie.

My birthday, which would probably be the only one I

would have this year, was twenty-four hours away. Actually, less than twenty-four hours, since I was born at five in the morning and it was already after six. And now I was ready to go out and follow the advice of the voice. I would *experience life.* Now if I only knew what that meant.

Nervous, yet filled with an exhilaration I had never known existed, I grabbed a few thousand peanut butter and cream cheese sandwiches I had hidden under my picture of a mattress for such an occasion, then tucked Hannibal safely under my arm.

"I am pleased no end that you've begun to use underarm deodorant."

"Who said that?"

"How many are there here, Winchell?"

"Only me . . . and . . . Hannibal? But how could you . . . ?"

"Telepathy, my good fellow. Didn't you read the last chapter?"

I went back and read it. She was right. She could communicate telepathically. It was nice to know I could talk with Hannibal, but at the same time, I couldn't be sure whether the thoughts in my head were hers or mine. My dad says that type of thing usually doesn't happen until you get married.

Once outside, I climbed down my one-step ladder. I picked out the largest apple I could find, stuffed it with every worm in our yard, and placed it in my baby robins' nest.

Next to the nest I left a book titled *How to Fly*. Figured it wouldn't hurt. Luckily, the first chapter included a section called "How Baby Robins Can Learn to Read This Book." I just hoped that it would keep them until I got back. Little did I know just how long that would be.

"If you want to get the full impact of your quest for experience, you must leave this domain completely," encouraged Hannibal.

"Okay. But first I want to experience . . .

THE CLIFF♪♩!"

"No," pleaded Hannibal.

She could tell me things, but she couldn't stop me. Sure, it was irresponsible of me. But I was a kid, and part of being a kid is that you gotta do what you gotta do. Know what I mean?

As Hannibal and I drew closer to . . .

THE CLIFF♪♩,

Hannibal tugged on my pants. Turtles of Hannibal's kind have this sixth sense of impending danger (although they fall far short in the five other senses).

"You know," Hannibal warned, "if you want to experience life before your birthday, you might want to make sure you still have a life to experience."

"Ah, you're just like my parents, except you're a lot shorter. They tell you to discover the world, then they don't let you cross the street."

You think a turtle was going to stop me? I ignored Hannibal's warning and walked right up to the edge of . . .

THE CLIFF ♫ ♩.

"Wow!"

The view was just awesome. From the edge of the cliff I could see the most beautiful spacious skies and amber fields of grain that I had ever seen. I mean, there was purple mountains' majesty for as far as the eye could see. And oh, that fruited plain. Just amazing! Isn't it weird how one person can stand on top of a mountain and see a wondrous view, while another person only sees how far down he might fall? I was one of those who didn't look down because it would have made me nauseous.

Of course, I wanted to get as close to the view as possible. Hannibal telepathically yelled for me to stay back a few feet, but unfortunately, being a smallish turtle, Hannibal's yell was more like:

 "Hey! Stay back a few feet!"

And anyway, Hannibal's telepathic powers only worked when the subject she wanted to telecommunicate with was within 4.75 feet.

As I inched closer to the edge of the cliff, a stiff breeze swirled by, so strong it felt as if I had been pushed. I lost my balance and before you could say, *"Hey, Winchell, watch out, you'll lose your balance and fall off the cliff,"* I lost my balance and . . . dear me, I fell off the cliff.

Hannibal, who had been busying herself with some tasty bugs, turned just as I fell.

She hurried to the edge of the darn cliff (as fast as a turtle can hurry) to see what I'm sure she wished she did not have to see.

With a large lump in her throat, Hannibal peered over. To her very, very pleasant surprise, about ten feet below, on a small but lifesaving ledge, there I was, holding my ankle.

"Hannibal! I think I broke my ankle. Hurry. Get help!"

Well, Hannibal didn't have to hear any more. There was no time to waste. I needed help and, gosh darn it, Hannibal would get it for me.

She turned away from the cliff and as fast as her four stubby little legs would carry her, she headed for my house. She kept repeating to herself, "Winchell needs help. Winchell needs help. Winchell needs help. Winchell needs help. Winchell needs help. Winchell needs help. Winchell needs help. Winchell needs help. Winchell needs help.

Winchell needs help. Winchell needs . . ."

SIX AND A HALF

Winchell Needs Help!

(This isn't really a new chapter,
but I've been told that shorter chapters are better.)

Hannibal hurried to get help. Inch by inch, she trudged on. The journey was, to say the least, tedious. Soon day turned into night, and still Hannibal lumbered on.

"Winchell needs help."

Night turned into morning and morning into afternoon. And, in what seemed like an eternity, afternoon turned into night again. Through snow and freezing temperatures, Hannibal plodded on. She knew that Winchell needed help.

Night turned into day and day into night. January turned into February (fortunately, not being Leap Year, February lasted only twenty-eight days), and February into March. At least it seemed like months. Fact is, it was actually about thirty minutes. But it was a long thirty minutes.

Now all this time I had sat, rather impatiently, waiting for Hannibal to return with help. And even though I had the utmost confidence in Hannibal, my birthday was fast approaching, and I figured it wouldn't hurt to try to get help on my own.

I yelled as loudly as I could:

"HELP!"

Wow. Being in pain and all, I didn't think I would be able to scream that loudly. Someone had to hear that. And someone did. Hannibal.

In all this time, Hannibal had been able to get only about thirty yards away.

Now remember, I told you that I was not one for learning, and one of the many things I had yet to learn was patience. Patience just takes way too long to get. Now impatience, that hardly takes any time at all.

"Even a turtle should be able to crawl faster than that," I cried. "You're not even trying!"

How thoughtless. Sure, I was in a bad spot, but still, you have to understand that others can have feelings too. Even others who are turtles.

And as if to ignore everything I just wrote in the last paragraph, I added, "Why, if I were a turtle, I would have gotten help by now."

The next thing that happened will be hard to believe, but I swear★ on my baby robins that it happened.

In what seemed like the blink of an eye, I was standing on the safety of the land overlooking the ledge and my ankle had miraculously healed.

I had no idea how it happened. But it didn't really matter as long as I was safe and sound and off that ledge.

"That's enough *experiencing life* for me. I'm heading home. Mom's gotta be awfully worried."

I took off as fast as my four stubby legs could carry me and my shell. . . . *Huh?*

Four legs? Shell?

I looked at my frightfully changed body. I hadn't been exercising that much recently, but I hadn't noticed that I was so out of shape. And the additional legs . . . That's gotta be more than just a lack of sit-ups.

If I didn't know better, I would have figured I had become a . . . *turtle?*

And where was Hannibal?

"Hannibal!" At least I had my old voice.

"I'm over here," chirped Hannibal.

Hannibal's voice seemed to be coming from over the cliff, where I had . . .

★ NOT BAD-WORDS "SWEAR," THOUGH I WAS CLOSE TO USING THEM, TOO.

I hurried over to the cliff as fast as my—oh, this is so hard to say—as fast as . . . my four stubby little legs could carry me. Which meant that . . .

Night turned into day and day into night, et cetera, et cetera.

Finally I reached the edge of the cliff and looked down. To my amazement, there I was, looking up at myself. Actually it was only my body looking up at me. Actually it wasn't me that my body was looking up at. It was Hannibal's body, or what used to be Hannibal's body, for now it was mine or . . . Geesh.

Fact is, some intense switching had gone on, and I was pretty upset. I couldn't wait to figure out who I could blame. But it wasn't long before I recalled that it was I who had first said, "Why, if I were a turtle, I would have gotten help by now."

Somehow, someone, something had given me the opportunity to prove my point.

"All right. I get it," I said to whoever or whatever was in charge of this absurd joke. "I've learned my lesson. Now give me back my body!"

But wait. This was going to be a little tricky. If the bodies were switched again, then I would be back on that ledge, and it would be years before Hannibal reached help, if ever. Geez, Louise. Experiencing life was not going to be as easy as I had thought.

I figured it might be better to stay in Hannibal's body and get help. I'd deal with the whole boy-to-turtle switch after my body was safe, sound, and rid of that rancid turtle smell that seemed to get worse with every step.

With a determined look, as much as a turtle can look determined, I set off to get help for Hannibal and myself.

SEVEN

Now What Do I Do?
Come on, Don't Just Sit
There Reading.
Answer Me!

(This is really a new chapter.)

My journey had just started, yet on this day I was to face a decision that would affect humankind as we knew it. And the fact that I hardly knew humankind didn't help.

"Wait a minute," I said to no one in particular.

The minute was finally over, and I realized it was time I started taking charge. I had to come up with a solid idea that could actually take me to where I wanted to go, fast. And it had to make sense.

Here was my *sensible* plan. If I could get hold of a time machine, I could go back to just before I fell off the cliff. I figured if just saying something could turn me into a turtle, coming up with a time machine shouldn't be a problem.

"Time machine appear!"

Nothing.

"Appear time machine!"

Nothing.

"Machine appear time!"

Okay, so I didn't have much of a grasp of how this wishing stuff worked.

I pretty much gave up, and then . . .

Zap!

I was going back in time! Not the seeing-things-from-the-past-whirling-by, movie kind of going back in time. This was real.

Unbelievable as it might seem to those of you who are reading this, I landed right next to . . .

THE CLIFF♫♩!

And it was definitely *before* I fell off of it. Unfortunately, I had underestimated the sense of humor of whoever or whatever was running this show.

If I was still a turtle, I had to be the tallest box turtle ever. Either that or my depth perception had been thrown way off by my travel through time.

Having no mirror available, I made my way over to the nearest watering hole to check out my reflection. I thought,

This place looks a heck of a lot like the late Cretaceous Period should look. (Coincidentally, the only school day I ever really enjoyed was when we went on a field trip to the Museum of Natural History.) But that would be crazy, because if this were the late Cretaceous Period, it would mean I went back ninety-eight million years.

I peered into the water, but I was unable to find my own reflection. The only image I could make out was some sort of brontosaurus. Not a gargantuan, ten-story-high brontosaurus like the movies would have you believe somehow end up in New York, eating their subway-fill of people. I mean, we all know that sauropods, of which the brontosaurus was one, were herbivores. The only people they would eat would have to have been made out of broccoli.

Anyway, this brontosaurus was only about fifteen or twenty feet high. It looked a lot bigger than the one I saw at the museum. This one actually had more than bones and . . . *a brontosaurus?*

I took off as fast as my huge, elephantlike, thick-skinned feet could take me, but I just couldn't seem to shake the fast-approaching giant. And while we now know the brontosaurus was an herbivore, I couldn't be sure if he knew that he was.

Whoa! Hold on there. What was I doing with huge, elephantlike wheels? While I never had the most flattering legs, the last time I had looked they were actually short, stubby, box turtle drumsticks.

Yikes! Not only had my legs changed, but I soon realized that the thunderous, earthshaking thumps of the brontosaurus were not coming from behind me. They were coming from *under* me!

I stopped and looked back, expecting to come face-to-face, or at least face-to-toes, with a colossal bronto-beast. But no. No brontosaurus. No nothing.

O-o-o-o-o-o-o-o-h. Uh-oh. (Whimpering here.) Now I got it. I swear this to be true. The reflection in the water had been me! This latest morph had caused me to become a full-fledged member of the sauropod family. But it's funny, this time I wasn't the least bit upset. In fact, I was downright thrilled.

I love dinosaurs. The stegosaurus, the *Tyrannosaurus rex*, and even the little known Elvisaurus (which some people think still exists) were all so cool. I certainly felt more comfortable with them than I did with those Neanderthal bullies at school. Especially that low-down, rotten Clayton Moore.

So being a brontosaurus wasn't so terrible. I decided to try out what I expected to be my most awesome roar.

"ROAR!"

Not bad, I thought. I bet I could scare the bejeebies out of—

"ROAR!"

Holy galopolins! What the hay was that?

Before me stood the most gargantuan, humongous, and quite large brachiosaurus I had ever seen. Of course, this was also the first brachiosaurus I had ever seen. At least in person.

I thought, How can I show this monster that he isn't messing with some spineless hayseed here? Of course, not being spineless made it much more difficult for me to cringe helplessly in my most defensive fetal position, waiting for the worst.

"Did you forget today's game or what?" roared the brachiosaurus.

Well, that had to be the last thing I expected to hear.

"The most important game of the season and you're just standing around like you're stuck in some tar pit. You want those stinkin' carnivores to win by forfeit?"

That was the next-to-the-last thing I expected to hear.

I had so many questions. How'd you guys become extinct? Were Adam and Eve before you guys or after? What game?

But before I could ask even one, the burly brachiosaurus grabbed me by my tail and dragged me through the heavy underbrush.

We came to a clearing where, holy moley, I was to see the most fantastic sight you could ever imagine.

EIGHT

Play Ball!

Before me stood a collection of dinosaurs that would have made even the most apathetic science teacher salivate.

There were triceratops, pterodactyls, megalosaurs, laelaps, spinosaurs, brachiosaurs, and velociraptors—like you would see in some great special-effects movie, except this was actually happening.

All of the 'saurs were positioned on a field, similar to the way baseball players are positioned on a baseball diamond. I'm not saying that it was actually a baseball diamond. That would be ridiculous. The distance from home to first base was ninety yards—much farther than regulation—so you know the baseball idea was a coincidence at best.

But darned if they didn't have nine prehistoric creatures on the field, and at least another nine in the visitors' dugout.

"Are you just going to stand there, or are you going to bat?" bellowed what was becoming a rather annoying but still very large brachiosaurus.

What could I say? It's not like I was going to tell him that baseball wasn't going to be invented for about ninety million years. Brachiosaurs hate to be questioned. Look it up. So I just grabbed a bat . . . er . . . uh . . . tree, and went up to the plate.

Standing out on the pitcher's mound was the meanest-looking *Tyrannosaurus rex* I had ever seen. I mean, I had faced tough-looking pitchers in Little League, but this guy made them all look like . . . well, like little kids, twelve and under. He was rubbing the ball in his claws and staring down at me.

I stared right back and waved my bat back and forth, ready to see his best. You just can't let a pitcher intimidate you, no matter how scaly his skin is.

He just sneered even meaner. Then he did the most disgusting thing I had ever seen in all my days as a brontosaurus. He snorted out this enormous glob of lunger (thick saurus spit) onto the ball and rubbed it in. Okay, now I was intimidated. It was repulsive, to say the least, and the worst part . . . it was totally legal. It would be millions of years before baseball would come to its senses and outlaw the spitball.

I dug in even more, gripping my bat so tightly that I could feel the prehistoric worms living inside struggling to breathe.

The *T. rex* wound up, whipping his arm, or whatever you call that appendage, with such an erratic motion that the last thing I expected was the slowest pitch I had ever seen: a knuckleball. Without knuckles yet! I was impressed.

The ball twisted and turned so many times, taking so long to get to the plate, that I had time to sign some autographs for the young stegosaurs butting horns near the dugout. I wasn't going to be one of those conceited superstar sauropods who didn't have time for the kids.

When the ball finally made it to the plate, it acted even more bizarrely, stalling in the air, right at the plate. Suddenly it started hopping up and down so radically that I was able to swing *three times*, missing it each time, before it reached the catcher's mitt.

"Strikes one, two, and three," screeched the umpire. "Yer out!"

That #&%@$# pterodactyl needed new glasses! How can you get three strikes on one pitch?

But then he pulled out the rule book and there it was, clear as day. Page 150, rule IV, paragraph 7: "A batter may take as many swings as he can per pitch and each of those swings is to be counted against the strike count."

It was known as the Primordial Ooze Rule.

I had struck out on one pitch! How embarrassing. But even so, things would get worse. Much worse.

The herbivores took the field. I was sent to right field. Even back then, I was a lousy fielder.

No need for me to go through what happened during the first thirty-six-and-a-half innings of this bite-your-nails, down-to-the-nub game since you can pick up that information at any good sports/paleontology bookstore.

It was the bottom of the thirty-seventh inning, and we were up 1–0. It was the most pivotal moment of my brontosaurial life.

There were two outs and the bases were loaded with about thirty-five tons of meat-eating speed demons. And they were razzing our pitcher unmercifully.

"Your descendants will become extinct!"

"Pitcher can't stand upright!"

"Your mother eats pterodactyl eggs!"

Actually our pitcher's mother did, in fact, eat pterodactyl eggs, so the carnivores' heckling was worthless.

The carnivores' manager, the cranky Matthew Goldin, asked for time and called the utahraptor back to the dugout for a pinch hitter. Not a smart thing. The utahraptor devoured Matthew in a single bite.

The assistant manager sent up a pinch hitter. The carnivore-partisan crowd roared as out of the dugout stepped a . . . gulp . . . *Gigantosaurus carolinii*! Yep. That's what I said. A *Gigantosaurus carolinii*. The largest dinosaur the carnivores had to offer. And a power hitter to boot!

This particular eight-ton theropod was considered the Cretaceous Period's top clutch hitter. Then I looked closer. There was something familiar about the batter. Not something you find in a dinosaur book. I couldn't place it. But then he shouted at me.

"Hey, Mink-a-dung! I gather you would appreciate asylum behind your *madre*'s apron right about now!"

Clayton Moore! I couldn't believe it. He had followed me into the past, and even as a dinosaur he was articulate. Drat. It made sense that he was a carnivore, but did he have to be their best player?

"After I secure this game, I will make you the main course for my next repast!"

Geesh. It was only around one o'clock and already he

was worrying about dinner. Was he obnoxious or what?

We countered by bringing in our top relief pitcher . . . Ogg. Og for short. He was an *Argentinosaurus huinculensis*, 130 feet long and 100 metric tons of mean with a fastball to match. Og might have been an herbivore, but his attitude was pure *T. rex*.

The stage was set. I moved way back. With my tail brushing against the fence, I was set to leap as high as I needed to stop any ball from going over my head and leaving the field.

For what seemed like hours, Clayton and the pitcher stared each other down. Seemed like? It was hours . . . literally. No wonder dinosaur baseball was a distant third in fan appeal behind soccer and evolution. It was slow and it was boring. So let me get to the meat of the story.

The count went full, and the stadium was all ahush as Og began his windup. There was a lump in everyone's throat, especially the utahraptor who had swallowed his manager. The manager was refusing to slide down into the dinosaur's stomach.

Og threw the fastest fastball I had ever seen. To be honest, it was so fast I didn't even see it. The only evidence that he actually threw the ball was what Clayton Moore did with it.

Clayton swung his colossal bat with a velocity only matched by Og's fastball.

The entire prehistoric world seemed to stop. Then . . .

Doink.

Clayton had missed the ball . . . almost. While our dugout erupted with cheers for the presumed out, the weakly struck ball was lifted into . . . right field! Stinky-player right field. *My* right field!

The only one with any chance to catch that ball and save the day was me. Lousy me. Horribly flawed, small-brained, brontosaurus me.

For a moment I lost the ball in the son. Not the *sun* . . . the *son*. As luck would have it, Og's son, a sizable *Argentinosaurus huinculensis* himself, who was wearing a white T-shirt and was seated in the stands directly behind the plate, stood up, obscuring my view of the ball.

Finally I caught sight of the sinking ball. Since I was way out by the fence, I would have to run my not-so-little tail off to reach the ball before it touched down to earth.

And did I run. I ran as if the fate of the world depended on that catch. In fact, it did.

NINE

The Big Bet

That's what I said. The fate of the world actually depended on whether I caught the ball. What I discovered around the twenty-fifth inning was that before the game, a bet had been made between the teams. If the herbivores won, life would go on as it had. If the carnivores won, all the dinosaurs would become extinct immediately. Today that would be considered a stupid bet. Back then it was called "adventurous."

The two runners who needed to score for the carnivores to win the game had already crossed home plate, and the ball was sinking faster than you could say "Watch out for the La Brea Tar Pits." As the ball was just about to hit the ground,

I knew I'd have to do something dramatic. I dove, using all 125 feet of my body length and 20 feet of my height, to reach out and . . .

"Yer out!" screamed the ump.

The ball seemed to have fallen safely in my glove, just a tenth of an inch from the ground. The next thing I knew, I was on the broad shoulders of the cheering herbivores who, by that time, had flooded the field.

Life would go on, I was the hero, and mighty Clayton had struck out . . . er . . . uh . . . flown out.

Everything was perfect. Except for one little thing:

I hadn't caught the ball!

I had *trapped* it. The ball had actually hit the ground before it went in my glove.

It was one of those plays that demanded instant replay, but in those days video cameras were in their infancy and weren't competent enough to be trusted in these big games.

The fact is, the only one who knew I had trapped the ball was . . . me. And no one else would ever know. That is, if I didn't say anything. And why would I?

It felt nice being the hero. Actually it felt great. I hadn't had much of a chance to be a hero millions of years later. Being popular felt good . . . real good. And there was always The Bet. If they knew I missed the catch, the carnivores would have won the game and all dinosaurs, of which I was one at the time, would become extinct. I'd have to be an idiot to admit to trapping the ball.

Just then my eye caught sight of a small diplodocus. Only about thirty-five feet long. A child. Kind of reminded me of myself when I was a young boy . . . or a young turtle. I forget what species I was at the time.

But I knew what that look was. It was the special look that a kid gives his hero. The one that says, "I want to be just like you." Then he gave me another look. The one that says, "Hey, dumbo, I saw you trap the ball."

Did he know that I didn't really catch the ball? Did it matter? And if he did know, was I letting him down?

If I didn't admit to my missed catch, I'd just be this hero who's not really a hero at all. I'd be one of those fake ones who care more about how they look than who they really are.

Then again, if I told the truth, that kid might have a solid foundation for a future based on authentic heroes. Of course, he'd also be extinct.

Reporters surrounded my locker.

"Ahem." The fake cough nearly stuck in my throat.

The reporters readied their note pads, waiting impatiently for my game-winning quote. I nervously opened my humongous jaws, ready to utter the words that might have had the greatest effect in all of history, when—

I was back. Back in the present. Not all the way back. I mean, I was still a box turtle, but I certainly was no longer prehistorically challenged.

I didn't even know what choice I had made. Had I done the right thing? What *was* the right thing?

I know dinosaurs are definitely extinct. But was it because of the game? Was it because I admitted to not catching the ball?

I certainly didn't want to be responsible for wiping out life as it was known. But then again, if I did, it brought us to where we are today. If the dinosaurs didn't become extinct, things would probably be a lot different. And can you imagine the poop? Um, maybe you shouldn't.

And what about the prehistoric Clayton Moore? Did I wipe him out? Is he extinct? I can't say that I would be upset if he had somehow found himself neck deep in the tar pits. It isn't easy being a kid . . . dinosaur . . . turtle.

It was getting late. And with no shut-eye, to speak of, for the past ninety-some million years, I needed to take a break. After all, Hannibal was still out on that ledge, and if I didn't get some sleep I'd never make it home.

I found a nice comfy patch of grass, drew my pruney, puny little head into my shell, and closed my beady little eyes for some much-needed rest.

TEN
Winchell Takes a Nap

ELEVEN

Winchell Wakes Up

(Editor's note: Actually Winchell woke up
a few minutes ago and he's still—
how can I put this tactfully?—in the bathroom.
We'll wait.)

TWELVE

Bobby Plungerbutt
(Back from the bathroom)

I was starting to get used to my new body. I didn't move much faster than Hannibal had, but I was beginning to appreciate some of the unique benefits of my circumstance.

My shell was a lot lighter than I had imagined. How many people get to bring their house with them wherever they go? Well, except for people who live in mobile homes. But this house, this shell, went wherever I went a good twenty-four hours a day.

I found the whole pulling my head in or out of my shell pretty cool. Head in. Head out. Head in. Head out. Head in. Head out. Head . . . Sorry. I got carried away for a moment.

I began to think that I was rather attractive, I mean, as much as a box turtle could be. Stubby legs? Heck. They were just sturdy.

My new positive attitude was kind of . . . interesting. As I continued my journey, even as a turtle, I was beginning to feel pretty darn good about myself. At least I was no longer a Mink.

It was just about this time that my life was to cross paths with one Bobby Dungermutt. Let me give you a little back story (to be sure, not a story about a back).

Way before this book was ever written, a poor plumber and his wife excitedly awaited the birth of their first and only child. The Dungermutt family was so excited. Oh, early in their marriage they did have a small hippopotamus named Lefty, but keeping his booties on wasn't so easy, and would you want to change a hippopotamus's diaper? I didn't think so.

For what it's worth, I'd like you to take a moment to really appreciate that last statement . . . the hippo and the diaper thing. Let it sink in real good. Finished? Helping change your little brother's or sister's diaper doesn't seem that bad now, does it?

Finally their little bundle of joy arrived, but, and I do mean *butt,* the otherwise normal Bobby Dungermutt was born with his rear end in the shape of a . . . *plunger.* No handle . . . just the plunger.

At first his parents were shocked, but within a few

moments, they fell in love. Bobby was their baby, and they were thrilled to have him. They wouldn't trade him or his curiously shaped butt for anything.

As the years went by, his dad would take Bobby with him to work. Bobby loved watching his father solve some of the great plumbing problems of the day. There was none better than Mr. Dungermutt when it came to pulling a toy from a stuffed toilet or rescuing some small, hairy mammal from a sink drain.

The love and joy Bobby received were returned tenfold. He would entertain his parents for hours on end with his incredible knack for flawless impressions of famous plumbing devices. Of course, he had an uncanny ability to suck up almost anything with his butt. Bobby's parents never had to ask twice for Bobby to clean his room. To Bobby, picking up toys was a breeze.

Everything was just swell, for the Dungermutts never paid attention to the insensitive neighbors who would whisper about the boy with the plunger-shaped fanny. These neighborhood rude-a-makers even took to calling him . . . Bobby Plungerbutt. Can you imagine?

As he grew older, Bobby began to feel that something was missing. For as much as he enjoyed spending time with his parents, there were no other children his age in the neighborhood. So when it came time for Bobby to go to kindergarten, he was very excited.

On this particular morning, an eager Bobby, wearing his best nonsticking-seat pants, skipped toward his first day of school. In fact he skipped right past me . . . in Hannibal's body, of course.

"Howya doin', Mr. Turtle?" called out the buoyant Bobby.

"Fine," I replied. "How are you doing?"

It all seemed so friendly. I didn't have the heart to tell him that Hannibal was actually a *Miss* Turtle.

"Have a great day!" Bobby shouted as he skipped on by.

Bobby seemed like a pretty nice kid, but with his inaccurate reference to my sex rolling around in my puny little box turtle head, I felt only disdain. Talk about being oversensitive.

Though Bobby was far out of earshot, I yelled out, "Nice butt, kid!"

That was rude. It was crude. What a crummy attitude. You would think, being uncoordinated and all, that I would be slightly more sensitive to someone else's . . . peculiarity. And, now being a turtle . . .

That's what you would think. But not me. Not then.

"I happen to be a perfectly attractive turtle. That kid was *weird*."

That was a mistake. Big time.

THIRTEEN

This Is a Switch

Talk about change. I found myself in a strange kindergarten class, and I wasn't in Hannibal's body anymore. No home on my back. No perfect little puny head. Not one single circle on my stomach.

I ran to the closest mirror. Immediately I realized that something was terribly wrong. First of all, I was able to *run*. Not like in *turtle* run. We're talking stand-on-two-legs *boy* run here.

In the mirror stood a boy. Not a *Winchell Mink* boy. But a Bobby Dungermutt boy. Butt and all.

I didn't know whether this was good news or bad. Actually it didn't matter what I thought. Once again I had changed and, as always, it seemed there was nothing I could do about it.

This time, though, something unusual happened. I not only looked different, but I also *felt* different. It's really hard to explain, but in any way you looked at it, I had become Bobby Dungermutt.

Being a turtle had been odd. Being a brontosaurus ballplayer was . . . different. This was downright screwy. But you know what they say:

"If you used to be a boy and then you're a turtle and then you're a boy again, just go with it."

Okay, I don't know if *they* actually do say that or even who *they* are, but it does make a weird kind of sense. I was so taken with my new situation that I completely forgot about getting help for my body, which was still stuck on that ledge.

Since it was the first day of school, some of the children were so nervous their knees were knocking. Some were rowdy. Some were assembling spitballs for later use. I had gone through kindergarten a couple of years ago, so I was feeling pretty darn confident. Feeling confident in school was new to me. I could have easily gotten used to this.

Fact is, everything was going splendidly. You know how it is in kindergarten. Nobody is really tough on you. Lots of cutting out stuff, pasting things on paper, learning the old ABCs . . . I was having a ball.

Unfortunately the fun was only temporary, for when the teacher left the room to do whatever it is teachers do when they leave the room, one of the rowdy boys finally noticed my butt. The boys started making fun of me, and the one making the most fun was Peewee Small.

Peewee was the tiniest boy I had ever seen. We're talking teeny. He wasn't much larger than a grape, though to be fair, I'm talking about a large grape. Kind of made me feel like squishing him. He teased me with things like:

"Hey, kid. Your butt looks like a plunger."

"Yo, Dungermutt, you got a plunger in those pants or what?"

It all seemed so peculiar, for no matter how odd my body might have looked, you would have thought that Peewee's little-bitty body should have made him more sensitive to being different. Shouldn't he have realized how much it hurts to be thought of as . . . irregular?

"Your butt is so-o-o odd," observed one kid.

"*Oui, mon ami*, your derriere is curiously distinctive," taunted Peewee articulately. A little bit *too* articulately if you asked me. There was something strangely familiar about Peewee. Something very *Clayton Moore*.

The mean-spirited comments didn't feel very good at all. In fact, they hurt bad. So bad that—and it's hard to admit this, being a guy and all—I began to cry. How embarrassing. Crying in front of a bunch of five-year-olds. I really hadn't been one for showing my feelings in public, but for some reason now I couldn't help it. And as I continued to cry, the other children teased me even more.

"Hey, Plungerbutt. Is that a tear in your eye or are you happy to see me?"

Well, now I felt even worse, for I had no idea what that meant. Not only did I have a butt to ridicule, but now I also felt stupid.

As I was about to run out of the classroom, Peewee tripped me. I fell to the floor so hard that, dread upon dread, I found myself *stuck*! Not just *stuck*, but STU-UCK!

My plunger-shaped rear end had taken a firm hold of the floor and refused to let go. That's when the teacher walked back into the room. Teachers always seem to show up a good second after you could have used them.

As hard as the teacher pulled, my butt just would not give.

You see, not only was my rear end in the shape of a plunger, but it was in better shape than the most excellent plunger ever made. I was stuck as no child had ever been stuck before.

Finally the custodian, feebly trying to hold back his laughter, cut out the floorboard, allowing me to get up. Now I was left with a new and further embarrassing addition. For you see, the only thing harder than concealing a plunger-shaped butt is trying to hide one with a healthy-sized section of floor attached to it.

After the custodian applied an entire can of WD-40 oil, my butt finally released the floorboard.

"I think it would be a good idea for you to go see the nurse and have her take a look at your buttocks," said the teacher.

Could she make the humiliation any worse?

In a flood of tears I ran out, being very careful not to fall or be tripped. The last thing I needed was to have my butt clamping itself to something else. Running was difficult enough as it was. Running with large pieces of junk stuck to your butt would be plain nasty.

But I didn't go to the nurse. All I wanted to do was get as far away from that school as I could. I headed for the Plungerbutt residence.

"You're home early," said Mother Plungerbutt.

"It's a time-zone thing."

"Wow. The things you learn in kindergarten today."

Then I ran upstairs. I was so mixed up and had absolutely no idea what to do. I prayed with all my might for my butt to be like everyone else's. Exhausted from the difficult day and all the extracurricular praying, I soon fell asleep.

FOURTEEN

A New Day. A New Butt?
(And the answer is . . . no!)

The next morning when I awoke, it was painfully evident that my butt had not changed. If anything, it seemed more plunger-shaped than ever. Another thing was evident. It had been fifty-five pages and I hadn't eaten a thing. Even if you're only a character in a book, you've got to eat.

"Bobby, that's your thirty-fifth plate of pancakes. Going to school creates quite the appetite."

Mrs. Plungerbutt obviously hadn't read any of this.

I definitely did not want to go back to that school. I had become the—no other way to say it—butt of everyone's jokes. Even the custodian had laughed at me. A custodian—

someone who had spent enough time with clogged toilets to know that a plunger is not something you laugh at, even if it *is* really a butt.

Then it hit me. While it had only been the first day of school for me, sooner or later I'd be moving on and Bobby would be back in his own body. He had about a zillion days of school left in his life, and if I let these creeps get away with this junk, Bobby's next twelve years of school would be just plain hell.★

I decided that I wasn't going to let Bobby take any more grief.

I went back to school with an attitude of fortitude. No one was gonna mess with Bobby again!

The teacher had yet to show, but it did seem much quieter than the day before. Too quiet. No class in the whole wide world would be that quiet when there was no teacher in the room. That was when some of the kids, led by Peewee, stood up.

"Hey, Plungerbutt. This look familiar?"

"Yeah, Plungerbutt. Whataya think of our butts?"

Oh, man! They had each strapped plungers to their butts. Having Bobby Dungermutt's expert eye for plumbing tools, I was able to recognize their plungers' inferior designs. Even so, I didn't even expect what was to come out of my mouth.

"They're not so bad. But, y'see, it's the butt you use for

★ SORRY, PARENTS. THERE JUST AIN'T A BETTER WAY TO PUT IT. ASK YOUR KID.

1at has the problem."

"What did you say?" steamed Peewee.

"Oh, I'm sorry. I guess it'd be really hard to hear when you're a—"

Everyone stared in disbelief 'cause I'm pretty sure they knew what was coming, but couldn't believe I would dare to say it.

"—butthead."

The rest of the class sat openmouthed. It was only the second day of kindergarten, but even in preschool, no one had ever stood up to Peewee. I think they kind of liked it. The whole standing up to a bully was a lot easier than I thought it would be, and it felt good. That was until Peewee got his ego up off the floor.

"I think ole Plungerbutt here needs to be taught a little lesson, guys."

Geez. Why was the teacher taking so long? I tried to throw Peewee off.

"You're speaking, of course, of some *school* lesson. Perhaps dinosaurs. I'm very good at dinosaurs."

"Very funny, Plungerdope."

Now he was getting personal . . . and physical.

"Here's your lesson. Let's get 'im, boys!"

From each side of the room, Peewee and three of his "boys" ran toward me with such speed that I only had time to duck.

Bam!

Wow. All four of them ended up in the center of the room, snarled in a heap; black, blue, and bleeding. The four of them being tangled up in one another looked kind of funny. A whole lot funnier than my butt. I couldn't help but laugh, and the whole class joined in. Well, except for the four bullies who were attempting to untangle themselves.

When they finally unraveled, you could see the smoke coming off Peewee's head. This kid was small, but when he got angry he might as well have been King Kong. Not that he got bigger. Just meaner. And since he was backed up by his kindergarten thugs, I thought it might be best if I took the rest of the day off . . . quick!

I ran out of the school with Peewee, his thugs, and the rest of the class close behind.

"What are you afraid of? We're just like you, Plungerbutt!"

Of course, I knew they weren't just like me. Cheap plunger workmanship aside, it's not like any of those kids had ever been a turtle . . . that I knew of.

As I ran, I noticed a tiny hole in the ground and stepped over it.

But for the size-challenged Peewee, it was near impossible for him to jump over the same hole. He made it about halfway across the hole, and that just wasn't good enough.

Down he went, as if the ravenous ground had swallowed his tiny body whole—like a dinky pea sliding into a straw, like an ant on a water slide, like a grain of salt on a rigatoni, like a . . . Sorry. I get carried away with metaphors. Or are they similes?

Like time standing still, everything and everyone stopped. No one had ever seen a kid fall down a hole before, especially this small a kid down this small a hole. It was frightening. When a cartoon character falls down a hole, it's kind of funny. But this was no cartoon character. This was a real-life, one-inch-tall boy. Even I forgot my problems for the moment.

Carefully, for they didn't want the ground to cave in, everyone approached the opening. They looked down into the deep, dark hole, but could see nothing but . . . a deep, dark hole.

"Are you okay, Peewee?" called out one kid.

There was no answer. Was Peewee hurt? Was he even— alive?

The entire school faculty came out to look in the hole. Even the laughing custodian, who was not laughing now, came to see if he could help Peewee.

Unfortunately the hole was so small that there was no way for anyone or anything to reach down into it.

The police showed up. The fire department showed up. Even the local news vans carrying attractive reporters with perfectly styled hair that refused to move in the breeze showed up. But no one could figure a safe way to get Peewee out.

The hole was so small that no piece of life-saving equipment had yet been invented to free Peewee. Engineers (not the ones with the trains) quickly calculated and determined that any digging around the hole could collapse it right in on Peewee.

It seemed, for the moment, that he might be doomed to a ghastly, stuck-in-a-hole type of death. If Peewee were still—*gasp*—alive, he might soon breathe his last tiny breath.

FIFTEEN

So Long, Peewee,
We Hardly Knew Ye

It looked like curtains for Peewee. Not the kind your mom hangs in the living room, unless, of course, you live in a funeral parlor.

Then, through the solemn crowd walked a boy, a boy with his rear end in the shape of a plunger!

I realized that I was put in this particular place for a particular reason, and my plunger-shaped butt had a particular purpose.

There was no time for embarrassment. I removed my pants, leaving on only a pair of dazzling blue tights that allowed my plungerbutt to do its best work.

This time there was no laughter, not even from the

custodian. There were only prayers. Prayers that asked that some way, somehow, Bobby Plungerbutt, who was really Bobby Dungermutt, who was really Hannibal, who was really me, would save Peewee.

I raised up and with the might of several rhinoceroses, I sat down on the hole, easily covering it fully and setting up a suction effect such as no one had ever seen before.

From the look on my face, you could tell that I was giving everything I had. The anxious silence was broken by a single sound—the voice of the custodian.

"Go, Bobby Plungerbutt! You can do it!"

Slowly but surely, one by one, other voices joined in: the kids, the faculty, the police and firefighters, even the reporters with the perfect hair.

"Go, Bobby Plungerbutt!"

"You can do it, Bobby Plungerbutt!"

"Bobby! Bobby! Bobby!"

For what seemed like hours, I gave everything I had until, finally, a great *POP* was heard.

Completely exhausted, I stood up. Lo and behold, stuck to my butt was one very weary but very relieved Peewee Small. A great cheer arose from the crowd followed by shouts of "We love you, Bobby Plungerbutt!"

I released Peewee and could hardly make my way through the cheering throng. Everyone was so thankful and happy, but none was happier than me. Oh, yeah, it's nice to save someone's life, but more important, the shouts of "Bobby Plungerbutt" no longer made me feel inferior. In fact, they actually made me proud. So proud, I had forgotten that I'd ever been a turtle or Winchell Mink.

To me, everything looked as rosy as things could look. Even the violets looked rosy. Even the weeds. Even the forlorn little box turtle standing off to the side looked rosy.

I picked him up and looked deep into his eyes.

"You're a pretty little turtle."

"I'm not pretty," shot back the turtle. "I'm handsome."

Winchell felt a great sense of closeness with the turtle.

"You look very familiar."

"I should," said the turtle with a smirk. "I'm you. I mean, you're me. I mean . . . Geez, keys, I'm all mixed up. What I'm trying to say is, I'm Bobby Dungermutt and you've got my body!"

That's when it hit me.

"Yes. Yes. I am. I mean, you are. I mean . . . Forget it. You know, Bobby, this body is quite comfortable, and I'm thinking that I just may stay in it."

"But that's not fair!" cried Bobby.

"Fair?" I shot back. "The only thing that's fair in this life is the one with a merry-go-round, crummy rides, and games that are impossible to win. Maybe you should get used to the turtle getup."

Zap!

At that point, or a second or two later (no one had a watch on so we'll never be sure), I found myself looking straight at Bobby . . . the boy Bobby. That's because, once again, I was back in Hannibal's body. Once again, I was a box turtle.

All I could think was, When am I going to learn to keep my big mouth shut?

(Note to Author: Write chapter about learning to keep your mouth shut.)

And what about Bobby? Well, the entire town learned that being different is not as meaningful as what you do with that difference. From that day on, wherever Bobby went, the voices, with Peewee Small's the loudest, exclaimed, "We love you, Bobby Plungerbutt!"

And you know what? They did.

A Commercial

We'll Be Right Back to the Book
After a Word from Winchell Mink.

Hi. I'm Winchell Mink. Whenever I'm not on one of my many adventures or telling you about them, I like to spend my time breathing. And I've found that there's nothing better for breathing than air. Now, you could use the air that you might find lying around the house or drifting about outside. But really, do you know where that air has been? People and animals you don't even know have been breathing that same air in and out. I mean, would you use someone else's toothbrush? That's right. Free air is filled with impurities and, worst of all, there's no profit in it for me.

That's why, when I need to breathe, I breathe
Winchell Mink's Fresh Air.

Bottled using only the cleanest mountain air, Winchell Mink's Fresh Air is the choice of celebrities and presidents of the United States (whom I'm not permitted to mention in this commercial).

And if you order a five-gallon container of Mink's Fresh Air right now, we'll include, at no additional cost, priceless old fingernails.

Hurry up and order before it's too late.

And now, back to the book.

SIXTEEN

So Nice to Run into Me

I was beginning to think that I would never reach home. Since I had become Hannibal, I'd been wandering for what seemed like years. Maybe it was only hours, but since it was extremely difficult finding a watch to match my shell, I'd probably never know for sure. Getting home before my birthday wasn't out of the question; which birthday it would be was a mystery.

But things were looking up. I had finally reached the halfway point of my journey. That's not to say I . . . uh . . . ever made it home. I certainly don't want to give away the ending.

Of course, only when I actually finished my journey

home would I know that this particular spot was halfway. Even then I would have to figure out the total distance, then divide it by two to get the actual halfway point. Way too much math.

Anyway, during this page, I actually passed the halfway point, so any more discussion is irrelevant.

And I would move speedily on to the next chapter if not for . . .

bam!

Not like *bam!* in some sort of comic book. I'm talking . . .

Bam!

When I came to my senses, I found myself on the ground. As I gazed about the accident scene, I couldn't believe what I saw. Me.

Not me. Another me. And not a mirror image.

An actual, real-live me. The old me. The boy me.

He was not only looking at me with the same baffled expression that I had, he was saying the same thing that I was. Listen . . .

Me: Who are you?

Other Me: Who are you?

Me: I'm Winchell Mink.

Other Me: I'm Winchell Mink.

Me: You couldn't be. I am.

Other Me: You couldn't be. I am.

Me: If you're me, how did I become a turtle?

Other Me: Do you really want me to go through the first half of this book again?

I certainly didn't want to waste my time, or yours, rehashing the whole zapping thing.

Me: How old will I be tomorrow?

Other Me: You mean, how old will I be?

Me: Whatever. Just answer.

Other Me: Twelve.

And to clinch it . . .

Other Me: And if you don't get back to your house before you turn twelve, you'll be a failure for the rest of your life.

I thought I had him there.

Me: Gotcha. You said, "you," not "I." If you were really me you would have said, "I'll be a failure for the rest of my life."
Other Me: Wrong-o. I am you, though I am a touch better looking.
Me: But why are you . . . ?

But before I could get another word out . . .

SEVENTEEN

Bam! Bam! Bam!

Hurricane winds began to swirl as Other Me and I were swept up in some sort of a spiraling tornado. It seemed like everything I'd ever seen in my life spun by. Toys, pets, Uncle Bert, an old half-eaten sandwich. I felt like Dorothy and Toto, or maybe it was the other way around.

"Hold on," said Other Me. "This ride ain't over."

Suddenly the winds stopped and we dropped like a ton of thick maple oatmeal. Slow, but tasty. It seemed like we fell for days.

I landed with a thud, although Other Me landed with kind of a tickly-bump-te-boom. Quite melodic.

Before I could take a breath, the skies went black. No stars. No moon. No nothing. Actually yes nothing (double negative, et al.). Just black. Like Mother Nature forgot to pay her electricity bill. She said she never received it, but big utility companies can be quite unforgiving.

It was quiet. Too quiet. If regular quiet were a fruit like an orange, this quiet would have been a watermelon. A really big watermelon.

Along with the quiet was a blinding whiteness as white as the quietness was quiet.

And then . . .

Bam!

Bam!

Bam!

Ouch! Man, that's gonna leave a mark.

Something . . . er . . . some thing*s* slammed right into me. When I was finally able to get my eyes used to the brightness, what I saw was to leave an impression that would last a lifetime. Or at least to the end of the book.

Standing in front of me and Other Me were three more Winchell Minks.

One by one they collected themselves. Total bewilderment crossed each Winchell's face as he realized he wasn't alone.

"Who are all of you?" we said as one.

"Well, who are all of you?" we responded as one.

After some fifteen minutes of us speaking at the same time, I finally couldn't take it anymore.

"Shut up!" I yelled.

"These are just a few of the many other you's who are all living their lives differently from you, though at the same time," explained Other Me. "It's a parallel universe thing."

"But I'm in the body of a turtle. None of you is a turtle."

"We never had to become turtles," said another me. "I chose to listen to my mom and not go near the CLIFF ♪♩."

"And long ago when people made fun of me," said another me who was overflowing with confidence, "I just didn't care. What made them so smart?"

I looked at the third me, who stood there defiantly. He looked like me all right, but there was something odd about him.

"What the heck are you looking at, creepo?" said the third me.

"Wha—?"

"Put your turtle eyes back into that dorky shell and shove off before I make turtle soup out of you."

He was a bully. I mean, I was a bully. I mean . . .

"And stop talking to yourself!"

And he could read my thoughts.

"I cannot, dumbo. You were thinking out loud."

How could I have become a bully?

"Y'see, turtle boy," he explained, "when I was about eight years old, my family moved into a new house. This jerk, Clayton Moore, started making fun of my name in front of a bunch of the neighborhood kids."

"Yeah. I remember that. He chased me down, gave me one heck of a wedgie, and hasn't stopped tormenting me since."

"Nah. I just told him that if he made fun of me one more time, I'd make sure that he'd be sorry he was ever born."

"And you're still alive?"

"Funny. No, he just apologized like the wimp he was and ran off. He never bothered me again. The other kids cheered. That felt pretty good."

"Standing up to Clayton and showing the other kids that they didn't have to worry about being bullied?"

"Nope. It made me realize that I could be an even bigger bully than Clayton. Nobody's messed with me since. Powerful stuff, huh?"

"Understand now?" said Other Me.

Not really.

That night we told one another about our adventures. Different places and times, different character run-ins, different transformations. None of the stories was the same. But there was something in each of us that connected.

We told what it was like for us before our adventures started. Odd as it may seem, our differences bonded us together.

We realized it was time to continue our separate journeys. We swapped e-mail addresses and promised to keep in touch. We never would, but it's something you do.

With a smile and a tear, all five of us bid adieu, good-bye, and in one case, shalom.

The whiteness fell away and I found myself alone, back where I first ran into Other Me.

As I crawled off into the distance, a thought kept running through my mind. I was the best-looking one of us.

EIGHTEEN

Honest Abe

I wished I didn't have to wear the shell. I wished I was the regular eleven-year-old boy who would never get picked for a team.

Do you know where wishing without doing anything about it gets you? No place. You'll be lucky if it gets you to the next paragraph.

Okay, you were lucky, but the point is, it seemed like I was never happy with who I was, even when I wasn't me.

Just then I saw a house like I had never seen before.

The first floor was where the second floor should have been. The second floor was where the third should have been. The third was where the first normally was.

The right side of the house was on the left and the left was on the right. Or was it the other way around?

The backyard was in the front of the house and the front yard was in the garage.

The welcome mat on the front porch read NO ONE WELCOME.

There were no windows and no doors. Seemingly no way in and no way out. Was the house built around the people who lived there, or were there no people inside at all?

Most unbelievable . . . there was hair growing on the roof! Not just a little, but so much that it had to be parted and braided.

A very odd place for sure, but perhaps one where there lived someone who could help me get my body off that darned ledge.

I was about to head for the front door when I found my nose smashed up against a pair of size eleventy-seven shoes. Size eleventy-seven shoes that still had someone in them.

I looked up and found myself staring at the largest man I had ever seen. From my turtle angle it would be difficult to determine his exact height. Let's just say he was tall-a-mondo. His towering stovepipe hat, gaunt face, and full beard made him look even taller.

His size would have normally freaked me out. But there

was something about him that calmed me.

He bent over and stuck out his hand.

"Hello, young man. I'm Abraham Lincoln. I hope you'll vote for me in the next election."

Whoa. Was this really Abraham Lincoln?

"Excuse me, but how could you be Abraham Lincoln? Didn't he die over a hundred years ago?"

"Give me a break, kid. You're a talking turtle who used to be a boy, and you're telling me that I can't be Abraham Lincoln?"

The stranger tried to prove who he was: "Born in a log cabin. Read by candlelight. Freed the slaves. Sixteenth president. Gettysburg address. Four score and seven years. Ford's Theatre, etc., etc., etc."

I tried to trip him up.

"How many years in a score?"

"Twenty."

Yep. He knew it all. This was actually Abraham Lincoln.

"I wonder if you might help me. See, my real body is stuck on a ledge and I—"

"That's not why I'm here, Winchell."

He knew my name.

"Before you ask for help from the people in this house, if there are any, there is something you should know."

"Sure. Go ahead."

"You better sit. This might take a while."

"I can't sit. I'm a turtle."

Lincoln began to tell me a story about the people who had lived in the house who . . . well, it might be better if I just let good ole Abe tell it.

NINETEEN

The Gratchkea

(Author's note: These are the actual
Abraham Lincoln transcripts.
They cannot be transferred or used in any manner
without the express approval of the Lincoln estate
and Major League Baseball.)

"In this house once lived an inventor and his family who were very poor. They couldn't afford a television or a radio to entertain themselves; no computer to surf the Net; no microwave to reheat the ice cream. And believe it or not, they didn't even have satellite TV.

"That's the bad news. The good news is, they lived in a time before any of those things were invented, so they never knew what they were missing. This normally would have been a good way to keep from getting a severe case of the *not-havings*. But not so for the inventor.

"Although he felt plenty blessed, the inventor wanted to do more for his family. He saw that other inventors' families

had bigger *things*. Bigger houses. Bigger food. Bigger chairs
. . . which of course they needed because when you eat all
that *bigger* food, sooner or later you'll need bigger chairs to
fit your bigger *you-know-what* into them.

"He hoped that one day he would come up with one
idea so big that he could afford to buy . . . bigger things.

"It wasn't that his family wanted more. They felt lucky
just having one another.

"I'm not saying this man was not a very good inventor,
but up till now he had either invented things that had
already been invented or he had invented things that didn't
work.

"Oh, there were times he invented things that kind of
worked and hadn't been invented yet. Unfortunately, they
were things that no one needed. Things like the flashlight
that operated only in the light; the rain-teller that could
detect rain if you just held it outside (if it became wet, it
was raining); or his most famous invention, the ice cube
defroster. I think you can figure that one out on your
own."

"Why does the house look so weird?" I interrupted.

"The guy built a flashlight that worked only in the light.
What kind of house do you think he would build? Now
may I continue, please?"

I nodded.

"One day the inventor had a dream. Not one of those

sleeping dreams, mind you. This was one of those *eyes-wide-open-wouldn't-it-be-neat-if-this-happened* type of dreams. He couldn't get it out of his mind. For this was a dream about an invention that the world had been waiting for. Of course, people didn't know they were waiting for it because it didn't exist yet. But when and if it were invented, I assure you they would be certain to say things like, 'We've been waiting for a thing like this all our lives.'

"It was the greatest idea any inventor ever had. It was . . .

the Gratchkea.

"All he had to do now was invent it. Of course, this is one of the most difficult parts of being an inventor. There are no instructions to follow. You have to *invent* those yourself. Which, I guess, is why they call them *inventions*.

"Anyway, the inventor set about to create his Gratchkea, and he had to hurry. What if some other inventor had the same dream? Worse yet, what if this other inventor were in an earlier time zone? He might have had his dream already and invented the wonderful Gratchkea a good two or three hours before our inventor.

"He would need complete privacy. He locked himself in his basement laboratory, which he had secretly hidden in the attic.

"How long he would remain there he didn't know, for when you create something that's never existed before, it's very difficult to figure out how much time it will take to build. This was an even larger problem before clocks were invented.

"But he had a job, nay, a dream, and that dream had to be fulfilled. He was sure that his family would understand and appreciate his effort.

"He worked day and night on his new invention. He didn't sleep. He didn't eat. He didn't even go to the bathroom. You don't drink or eat and this will happen. All he could think of was the Gratchkea.

"Soon he began to miss out on family events. He missed his wife's birthday, but he was sure she would forgive him, for when his Gratchkea was sold he would have enough money to buy her extra birthdays, which she could celebrate anytime she wanted.

"He missed the annual Cub Scout father-and-son weenie roast, but he knew one day his son would understand. For when the Gratchkea was finished, he would be able to buy weenies for every Cub Scout in the entire world.

"Finally his daughter's dance recital passed without him attending. This was the memorable production in which she played the role of the lead tree in the J. K. Rowling Elementary School presentation of *Rain Forests Are All Wet*.

"Again, he knew she would soon appreciate how important his work was. When the Gratchkea became a must for every household, the inventor could afford to put an armed guard next to every endangered tree in that damp old rain forest.

"And so his work continued. The Gratchkea was taking shape, but it would need more time. Days became weeks. Weeks became months. Months became month and a halves. Point is, time was passing and still the Gratchkea wasn't finished. There were problems.

"First the widgets wouldn't fit into the kreplochs. Then the breslinks ruptured when he tried to resize them for expected spillover. And when the quiplerslits exploded all over his new lab coat, well, you can just imagine the mess.

"But as any good inventor worth his Bunsen burner knows, you have to expect problems. If it were easy to invent things, then who would need inventors?

"So, despite the frustrations and disappointments, he pushed on. The Gratchkea was going to be a success and so would he.

"The inventor was nearing completion of the Gratchkea and, thankfully, no one else had yet beat him to it. He was sure it would all be worth the trouble. His family and the whole world, for that matter, would be forever thanking him.

"Unbeknownst to the inventor, his family could not wait any longer.

"His wife, getting up there in age, was moved to a cheery senior citizens' home where she drew praise for water ballet and her stylish oven mitt designs (which became all the rage when she was bought out by The Gap).

"The son established the now-famous worldwide chain of Blockbuster Weenie Boutiques, which he ran with his wife and three children, a boy and a girl.

"The inventor's daughter, after receiving five Academy Award nominations, actually won one for her starring role in *Rain Forests Are All Wet, the Sequel*. But she found no happiness with it, as it fell on the eve of her seventh divorce.

"Meanwhile, back in the laboratory, the inventor bolted the final flangebit on the rounded z-cycle clip, and lo and behold . . .

"It was done! The Gratchkea was, in fact, now . . . factual!"

TWENTY

It's a Gratchkea World

(Honest Abe continues.)

O f course, any invention is not truly complete until you try it out to see if it works. The same goes for the Gratchkea.

"With a nervous hand and a hopeful heart, the inventor flicked the Gratchkea's switch. He waited for what seemed an eternity, for as we know today, a Gratchkea takes a bit of time to warm up.

"And then . . . and then . . . it turned on! The Gratchkea worked! It really did!

"The inventor ran as fast as he could down the stairs. Everything he and the family would ever want could now be theirs.

"'The Gratchkea works! The Gratchkea works!'

"But hold on here a minute.

"Where was everyone? Where were his wife and children? Now that the Gratchkea was finished, the inventor would be able to spend the rest of his life with his family enjoying the fruits of his labor. But his family was nowhere to be found.

"As he searched the house, he caught sight of a picture depicting the profile of a very old man. He turned toward the picture, and gosh upon gosh, the old man in the picture turned toward him.

"It was not a picture at all. It was, in fact, a mirror. And the old wrinkled face in the mirror was his.

"How did that happen? When did he have the time to get so old? It couldn't have been that long since he started work on the Gratchkea, could it?

"He collapsed on the couch. No wife. No son. No daughter. No family. Only a Gratchkea by his side.

"Pretty sad story, huh?"

Mr. Lincoln sat there, a tear running down his long, drawn face. I was feeling pretty darn bad myself.

"What happened then?" I asked.

"That's it, Winchell. That's exactly how this story ends. A man and his Gratchkea . . . together, and alone."

"Geesh. That's pretty sad."

I mean, he did have the Gratchkea. But it didn't seem to

make him very happy. And now he was really alone.

"Was it worth it? Could the Gratchkea replace a family?"

"Good questions," said the smiling late president.

"Thank you." Back then I would pretty much take anything as a compliment.

"How romantic do you think his next anniversary dinner would be, alone with the Gratchkea?" the Honest Abeman asked. "How many father-and-Gratchkea weenie roasts do you think there would be? There was no way any Gratchkea would be able to give a decent rain-forest tree performance. It dawned on the inventor that—"

"Wait a minute," I interrupted. "I thought you said that was the end of the story. You know, a man and his Gratchkea . . . together, and alone."

"No, I didn't."

"Yes, you did."

"No, I didn't."

"Yes, you did. Check the last page."

Lincoln checked.

"Okay, you got me."

"I thought you never lied."

"That was Washington. I'm the rail-splitter. Anyway, this wasn't a lie. I was just trying to make the story a little more dramatic."

He continued.

"Something dawned on the inventor! One of the little extras that he had built into the Gratchkea was a time machine, complete with a youtherizer. A youtherizer makes the Gratchkea's passenger as young as he was at the time he returns to."

"Whew, what a lucky break," I said.

"Now mind you, this wasn't one of those great time machines that allow you to go back to the Middle Ages or anything like that. But it could get you back a good forty or fifty years.

"The inventor quickly set the time machine for just moments before he had made his fateful decision to invent the Gratchkea, and back he went.

"He went back to before he lost his family and his happiness. Back to exactly the time he had The Dream. Not one of those sleeping dreams, mind you. This was one of those *eyes-wide-open-wouldn't-it-be-neat-if-this-happened* type of dreams.

"With a smile, he said, 'Nah. I don't think so.' He went over to his pleasantly surprised wife and children and kissed them all. And they lived happily ever after."

I waited for a second. It seemed like "happily ever after" was a proper ending to the story, but Lincoln had fooled me before.

"Is that it?"

"Yes. That's it. What do you think?"

I actually wasn't sure what I thought. I mean, I was feeling something. Something different. Something . . . comfortable. I sensed that whoever I was, whatever I had, was just fine, even though I actually still wasn't my old self and I didn't seem to have anything but a shell.

"It's still all a bit confusing," I admitted. "But it really makes me think about not wanting to end up alone, with only a Gratchkea to love, or a Gratchkea to love me. Maybe I had better think hard about what's really important in my life. Like, sometimes it's not what you get. Maybe it's more about what you lose."

"Very good, Winchell. Very good."

"Thank you."

When I looked up, I found there was no one there to thank. Lincoln had vanished. But I really couldn't stop thinking about the Gratchkea. What I couldn't stop thinking about was that if the inventor didn't invent the Gratchkea, where did the Gratchkeas come from that are so popular today?

"Oh, yeah . . . the Gratchkea."

It was Lincoln's voice. No body. Just the voice. And once again he hadn't finished his story.

"You know how popular Gratchkeas are today, right? Well, unbelievable as it may seem, remember that inventor in the earlier time zone that our inventor friend was afraid would invent the Gratchkea before he did? That's exactly

what happened. Seems like he finished his Gratchkea a good ten or fifteen minutes before our inventor would have finished his. So all and all, not attempting to invent the Gratchkea became one very happy tale, and I swear, it all happened just the way I said."

"What about me getting help from the people in the house?"

"No one lives there now," responded Lincoln. "It's been on the market for fifteen years. They're asking way too much."

And that was it. I never heard from Lincoln again. I've written him many times since. You know, at his Gettysburg address, but the mail always comes back with MOVED, LEFT NO FORWARDING SPEECH stamped on the envelope.

TWENTY-ONE

A Jury of Someone Else's Peers

By this time I knew that getting home was not going to be an easy task. I also understood I had no choice. I mean, of course, I still had some choices. I could eat grass or I could eat some disgusting bug that still had plenty of squirm left in him. But when it came to how I should live my life, the only choice was to reach home, get someone to pull my body off the cliff, and use what I'd learned to make a go of life. And there wasn't anybody who could stop me from doing just that.

"Pull over, buddy."

Startled, I turned to find two rather buff box turtles, both wearing some kind of police or military uniforms.

One wore a sombrero, the other a fez. Or was it the other way around?

"Can we see your identification, please?" said the larger turtle, who was wearing the fez . . . or the sombrero.

"What identification?" I replied. "I'm a turtle. I have no pockets. Where would I carry identification?"

"I'm afraid we're going to have to ask you to come with us," sneered the turtle that I'm pretty sure was wearing the sombrero.

On the trip downtown I tried to explain that I had left my wallet in my other shell. But the two officers couldn't have cared less, being too busy passing their hats back and forth, trying to confuse me.

They had heard it all before. Drunken turtles. Turtles with records as long as your arm. Turtles on the lamb (although the lambs were kept in separate cells). They had learned long before that a box turtle would say anything to get out of going to jail. They figured I was no different.

I was led into a holding cell filled with all kinds of turtle scum. No turtles. Just their scum. You would think they would clean the place once in a while.

"You've got the wrong turtle, I tell ya! Y'dirty rotten coppers," I shouted, quickly falling into traditional movie jail jargon.

Upon closer inspection I found one other occupant in the cell—a rather crusty-looking old maggot blowing on a harmonica. He was playing some sort of Broadway tune. You know, the kind you've heard before but can never remember the name of. He kept playing that same annoying song over and over. I was going out of my mind. Not only couldn't I remember the name of the song, but it was one I hated. Worse, I only knew one line from the song, so that was all I could sing.

The maggot finally pulled the harmonica from his lips, yet unbelievably, the music continued to play. Seems that he had actually never been playing the harmonica. There was an old tape player sitting behind him and that's where the harmonica music came from. The maggot was a phony. How I hate phonies. I hate them even more than the awful song that continued to play.

"Time for your trial."

It was the officer who had brought me in.

Trial? What trial? I hadn't even been told what I was arrested for and I was already going to trial?

"What kind of legal system is this?"

"Needs a little work, don'tcha think? We got it from the marsupials, and I don't have to tell you how corrupt they are."

I couldn't argue with that.

He brought me into a room that I guessed was the courtroom, but it was different from any I had ever seen.

There was a large bench toward the front of the room

where a judge was to sit. Next to that were a witness box and chair. To the right were twelve chairs set for a jury. In front of the judge's area were tables for lawyers that . . .

Hold on. It was *exactly* like what I had seen before. Except, of course, for the mouthwatering dessert table with a complete make-your-own-sundae section set up next to the guillotine.

Guillotine?

Seems that this particular court had the trial, last meal, and punishment positioned precisely so as to have the most time-efficient justice system in all the world. It was *guilty, gorge, and good-bye.*

I was told to sit in the defendant's chair. Sitting next to me was my attorney, a young but enthusiastic public defender tortoise by the name of Danny Webster. He patted me on the shoulder sympathetically.

"This is going to be a toughie, Mr. Mink, but I swear to you, I will do everything in my power to keep you from having to visit that dessert bar."

"Can you tell me what I'm on trial for?"

"You mean you don't know?"

"No, I don't."

"Gulp."

"What do you mean, 'gulp'?" I asked.

That's when my attorney revealed his strategy.

"I don't know either."

"All rise," proclaimed the bailiff. "The Honorable Clayton T. Moore presiding."

In walked this large box turtle whose face looked strikingly similar to—here we go again—Clayton Moore's. It was probably just a coincidence. Lots of turtles could have the name Clayton Moore and look just like him.

"Will the Stink-a-dink please rise," commanded Judge Moore.

"The name is Mink," I corrected.

"ORDER IN THE COURT!" bellowed Judge Moore as he pounded his gavel made from the shank bone of a velociraptor fossil.

"Mr. Pinky Fink. This is my court and I will call you anything I please. Is that clear?"

I nodded solemnly, thinking that the chances of this judge being related to my Clayton Moore were getting better and better.

"Are you familiar with the charges, Mr. Mink?" asked Judge Moore.

"No, I'm not."

"Good. Bring in the jurors."

The twelve turtles who made up the jury entered the room and, to my great surprise and even greater concern, they too looked exactly like Clayton Moore.

"Why do the jurors look like that?" I asked Webster.

"Couldn't tell you, Mr. Mink. Jurors all look the same to me."

"Will the prosecutor please state his case," directed Judge Moore.

I cringed as my own attorney, the young Danny Webster, stood up.

"I'm ready, Your Honor."

TWENTY-TWO

The System Works.
Unfortunately, Not for Me

To say that I was shocked would be, well, true.

"You're the prosecutor *and* the defense attorney?"

"Budget cutbacks," Attorney Webster admitted. "The court system has been quite low on funds lately, so that, frankly, we've had to consolidate a number of jobs."

"But how can you defend me and prosecute me?"

"To the best of my ability, Mr. Mink. To the best of my ability."

This couldn't get any worse.★

Webster continued. "Your Honor, the defendant has been charged with the most heinous crime a turtle can be accused of."

★ WHEN SOMEONE IN A STORY SAYS THAT THINGS COULDN'T GET ANY WORSE, THERE'S AN ALMOST 100 PERCENT CHANCE THINGS WILL DO JUST THAT.

"I thought you said you didn't know what I was charged with," I whispered.

Webster leaned over to me. "I was speaking then only as your defense attorney. What kind of prosecutor would I be not to know the charges? That would be laughable."

I wasn't laughing.

Webster approached the jury. "Members of the jury—"

"And a handsome jury they are," interrupted Judge Moore.

"Members of the jury," Webster continued. "This so-called turtle has committed a crime against all turtlekind."

The entire jury leaned forward.

"The crime of . . . *body snatching!*"

Cries of shock filled the courtroom. Cameras flashed. Mothers hid their children's eyes. The children would spend the rest of the afternoon trying to find them. I sat in stunned silence.

"Your Honor, the body that sits there surrounding the defendant does not belong to Winchell Mink, but to Hannibal Fip. Ms. Fip, a once proud and still innocent Mystical Turtle, now sits painfully on a ledge attired only in the grotesque and out-of-shape body of the defendant."

The jury, severely shaken by the sordid description of my human body, one even throwing up the previous day's already digested bugs, swiftly jotted down the horrid details.

"But I never asked for the bodies to be switched!" I cried out. "And what do you mean, 'out-of-shape'?"

"Sit down, you vile and obviously guilty human in turtle's clothing," admonished Judge Moore.

"And you call this a fair trial?" I roared, though it came out as more of a whimper. On the other hand, Judge Moore was spitting fire.

"First of all, Minky-dink, you were never promised a *fair* trial. Second of all, if you are innocent, which I thoroughly doubt, the jury will find you innocent. Of course then I'll have them put to death. DO YOU UNDERSTAND?"

"DON'T YOU YELL AT ME, YOU BIG UGLY BLOWHARD," I threatened, though it came out as more of a "Yessir."

"Mr. Webster, call your first witness," ordered Judge Moore.

"If it pleases the court, I call to the stand Winchell Mink."

"Are you the prosecutor now or my attorney?"

"Can't be sure, Mr. Mink. Things move very quickly here."

I stepped into the witness stand. The bailiff approached.

"Put your hand on this leftover piece of horsefly carcass, please."

Gingerly I placed my hand on the horsefly carcass,

which, oddly enough, had a number of horseflies buzzing about it.

"Do you promise to uphold the tortoise creed," recited the bailiff, "admit to your guilt, and buy lunch for the court officers, so help you God?"

"Does it matter where I get the lunch from?"

"That's up to you. We try not to put a lot of unnecessary demands on the defendants."

"Then I do."

Webster approached the stand. "Would you state your name for the record?"

"Winchell Mink."

"Do you have any proof of that?" asked Judge Moore.

"Not on me, but I can prove it. Call my name."

"Winchell Mink," called out the perplexed judge.

"What?" I responded quickly. "See. Only someone named Winchell Mink would answer to that name."

Judge Moore thought a bit, then nodded. "You may continue."

Webster went nose to nose with me. "Have you ever stopped being guilty of this crime?"

"Yes."

"You mean you once were guilty?"

"No, I mean—"

"And wouldn't you agree that if someone were once guilty, he would have to always be guilty? You can't just decide not to be guilty, can you?"

"No . . . Yes . . . I don't know. I'm so confused."

"I rest my case," declared Webster.

"Your Honor, I object!" he quickly added.

"Objection overruled," bellowed Judge Moore. "Ladies and gentlemen of the jury, have you reached your guilty verdict?"

"We have, Your Honor," they announced with way too much enthusiasm. "We find the defendant . . . extremely guilty!"

I wasn't exactly surprised by the decision. In fact, before the jury foreman had opened his mouth I was at the dessert bar scooping my first dish of Death by Chocolate ice cream.

"Do you have anything to say before I pass sentence?" asked the Judge.

"Yes. Yes, I do."

I climbed up on top of the make-your-own-sundae bar, and even I couldn't believe what I said.

"I accept the jury's decision. I find it fair and just. I have taken Hannibal's body. I don't know how, but I'm pretty sure I know why."

"And why is that?" probed Judge Moore.

"It's hard to explain, but perhaps I can do it with a song."

With that I pulled out a hat and cane and turned toward

the orchestra that was to be put on trial next.

"Hit it, boys!"

With a flourish, the band struck up. And with it I began to sing.

(Sung to the tune of Mozart's Unwritten Concerto in the Key of Car. . . . The Car Key.)

♪♫♩ *"I was just a boy with no place to go,* ♩♫♪
My life was sad and my head hung low,
I wished that I didn't have to be me,
Now I know me's the only me to be."

I finished the song, but I still went for the sympathy vote: "If you put me to death, you will certainly be doing the same to the very innocent Hannibal."

As a single tear trickled down my cheek (nice touch, don'tcha think?), the entire courtroom went nuts. I mean, just imagine! A defendant admitting his guilt so melodiously and, in doing so, understanding that his crime could actually have a positive impact on his life. It was, to say the least, unique.

Turtles who hadn't ever received a single dance lesson were spinning and jumping with such skill that even the most overpriced dance teacher would be impressed.

Turtle eggs that had yet to hatch were spinning in perfect symmetry.

The jury quickly reversed its guilty decision and, just as quickly, laid down a section of ice, slipped on ice skates, and skated to a choreographed number that would have put *Disney on Ice* to shame. As part of their routine, the same twelve turtles who moments ago had ruled against me were now lifting me high over their heads, screaming out, "We were wrong! We were wrong! Please forgive us in a song."

And I did.

♪♪♪ *"Of course I will forgive your wrong,* ♪♪♪
And I just did it in a song."

I finished with a bow and a wave that would have been the envy of Miss America, if Miss America were a turtle.

As one turtle placed a crown on my head, another handed me a bouquet of long-stemmed roses.

I looked ridiculous, but justice had been done. All would be well.

TWENTY-THREE

Order in the Court!
Okay, I'll Have a Tuna on Rye
(Sorry. Couldn't Resist.)

While all this was taking place, Judge Moore was beside himself, and the two of him banged his gavel.

"Order in the court! Order in the court! This has all been most extraordinary. While it is my personal preference to do away with the defendant, I must consider that I am running for mayor next year and need your vote. As a political candidate, doing what I think is right is not nearly as important as doing what will get your vote. Therefore, I feel I have no choice but to release Mr. Link-a-dink-a-doo."

The courtroom erupted in cheers. But no one was

happier than I. I could now complete my journey.

"I'm only kidding," interrupted the judge with a chuckle. "He still has to face the guillotine."

But one member of the jury shouted out. "What about Hannibal?"

Once again the court fell silent. He was right. With all this hubbub, everyone seemed to forget about the real victim here.

"She's still out on that ledge stuck in that disgusting human body."

I cringed. It may have been disgusting to these handsome reptiles, but it was my body, and the sooner I climbed back into it, the better. I raised my hand.

"Yes, Minkle-dinkle-finkston-winkle. Do you have to go to the bathroom?"

"Yes, I do."

Being a turtle, my knees were pretty far apart, but still I tried to bang them together in what was a useless effort to hold off the much-needed bathroom dash.

"But before I go, I wanted to bring up one point. If you will release me to complete my journey, I make a promise to you. I will return to that ledge to not only rescue Hannibal and my disgusting human body, but also transform her back into a turtle. How I will do this I do not know, but there was *something* that sent me on my journey. That *something* will understand that my quest has reached its conclusion and, I would hope, return the two of us to our original forms."

Shouts of "Let him go" filled the courtroom, and Judge Moore finally relented.

"All right, all right. I'll let him go. Just shut up! Winchell Dink-a-fink, you were lucky this time. But I swear, you haven't seen the last of me. And I promise, no matter where you are, no matter what you do or what form you take, you will not be able to hide from me. I will pursue you to the ends of the universe and I will make sure that your life is a veritable *h-e-double-hockey-sticks* on Earth. Do you understand?"

I just smiled and gave the *okeydokey* sign.

And with that, the courtroom suddenly disappeared along with all the turtles in it. All that was left was me . . . and my journey.

Did any of that really happen? Was it all a dream? Was it just a bunch of words, sentences, and paragraphs that some hack writer needed to fill enough pages so that his publisher wouldn't reduce his pay?

Alas, there was no time to sit and ponder the possibilities. Hannibal, and my body, needed help.

TWENTY-FOUR

The Birds

(Tee-hee)

The whole trial thing had thrown me way off course.
I had no idea where I was and which way I had to go
to reach home. I was lost and, once again, alone.

Chirp-chirp-chirp.

I looked up and . . . *plop!* I took a mess of bird schmutz
right in the eye. That was the bad news. The good news?
That schmutz came from a group of robins. My robins.
The ones who lived outside my window. They were flying
like old pros. They had obviously read the *How to Fly* book
I left for them.

Chirp-chirp-chirp-chirp-chirp.

They were flying in a kind of arrow formation. I wasn't

a robin, but I knew these birds well enough to know what they were telling me. Hey, I raised those kids. They were saying, "Follow us!"

And I did. I followed for quite a while. I don't know how long, but there came a time when I reached a gate. A familiar gate. When I looked through the gate, what lay before me was the most beautiful sight I had ever seen . . .

Home.

TWENTY-FIVE
Home, Finally . . . Kind Of

Whew! Finally. My house never looked so good. I didn't care that it had no ceiling, no floor, and only three walls. I didn't care that we had only pictures of furniture. I didn't even care that my name was Mink. My journey was almost at an end. My goal was in sight. Soon I would be able to get Mom to help rescue my body and Hannibal's soul, still on that ledge.

With renewed enthusiasm and all the might I could muster, I set sail for the house. And, well, you know, a couple of months later, I reached the door.

I took a long, deep breath, rose up on my two hind legs, and was about to knock on the door when . . .

Someone lifted me up.

It has to be Mom, I thought. Beautiful Mom.

This certainly wouldn't be the first time I was wrong. And it also wouldn't be the first time I would have to deal with . . .

Clayton Moore!

He lifted me up to his face.

"Hel-loo, Winchell."

Why wasn't he extinct along with the rest of the bully carnivores? Why didn't he disappear along with the rest of the turtle court?

"Did you enjoy your journey?" He smirked.

It was all I could do to hold back from cussing out that slime. Not that Clayton could understand good old turtle profanity, which only common decency prevents me from using here. But Cheez Whiz and crackers, hadn't Clayton done enough? Couldn't he leave me alone just this once? Did he have to be so crummy 100 percent of the time? Of course, the most important question of all was: What is the capital of New Hampshire?

Answers: No. No. Yes. Concord.

"I think you'll enjoy this little diversion I have planned for you." Clayton smiled.

I had a hunch that Clayton was being sarcastic. Then again, people can change. I definitely had . . . more than a few times.

Could Clayton Moore have seen the evil of his ways?

"I can't wait to see your beady little eyes pleading for mercy," Clayton sneered.

Another theory thrown out the window.

Clayton carried me off, and as I watched my house disappear in the distance I couldn't help but think that perhaps my journey had been an outright waste. When I saw where Clayton was taking me, I was sure I was right.

Twenty-Six

The Class Cutup

There it was. School. The last place I wanted to end up. And I had this sneaking suspicion that it might really be the *last place*.

This is going to be so embarrassing, I thought. It's bad enough being a Mink, but now my whole box turtle getup will make me a genuine laughingstock, and not a stock that anyone would want to invest in.[*] I was not only back in school, but I was in biology class. My absolute worst subject. I would rather die than sit through a biology class. Especially today, when they were doing that disgusting dissecting.

Dissecting?

---

[*] I'VE BEEN TOLD THAT REFERENCES TO THE STOCK MARKET AND INVESTMENTS WILL ATTRACT READERSHIP THAT MIGHT WANT TO FINANCE MY NEXT BOOK, *HOW TO MAKE MONEY WITHOUT HAVING TO DO A WHOLE LOT.*

You have got to be kidding. Do you believe this? There they were, the entire class, with these poor little froggies pinned down helplessly in those dissecting pans. *Illlch!* How unfair. How inhuman.

Well, at least they're not dissecting box turtles today, I thought.

"Clayton," greeted my teacher, Mr. Pringle. "You found a box turtle for us to work with. Good job."

What did he mean, *work with*? Did he mean that he wanted to do some joint venture with the class and me? You know, having the class learn how to collaborate with small, tortoiseshell creatures.

Yeah, that's it, I thought. He wants to teach them teamwork. Teamwork with slow, hard-shelled reptiles. It's a great idea. It'll get them ready for the corporate workplace. I love it!

"Now Clayton, remember to carefully slice the turtle's body and tissue away from the shell," instructed Mr. Pringle. "We don't want to get too much blood on the carcass."

Another one of my theories shot to pieces.

"What about teamwork?" I shouted. "Come on, guys, teamwork is good and nowhere near as messy."

They acted as if they didn't hear, because they didn't. See, box turtle shouts don't exist. Not to Mr. Pringle. Not to the rest of the class. At least not in this chapter.

"Yeah, right." Clayton laughed.

Clayton must have had some sort of turtle-translation, thought-reading device. Either that or somehow Hannibal's telepathic powers had transferred to me.

Helpless, I was carried to his desk, where I was prepared for the extremely yucky surgery. I was doomed.

"Where's the great 'Winchell needs another lesson in morphing' now?" I pleaded with whoever was in charge of my morphing episodes. "This is when I really need it!"

Clayton readied his knife.

"What about chloroform?" I implored. "Have you no mercy? Where's your humanity? Where's the Novocaine? Where's the mask? Even traitors get masks! Haven't you ever read about Benedict Arnold?"

I figured a historical reference, one suggesting the birth of our great nation, might stir a bit of patriotic compassion in Clayton. But it didn't work.

"This is not antipatriotic, Mink-a-dink. This is just plain fun." Clayton smirked.

This Clayton fellow wasn't a boy. He was a monster!

All I could do was close my beady little eyes and wait for the inevitable. I knew I was a goner because my life started passing before my eyes.

In the womb. The placenta. The embryo. The . . .

Whoa there. I had gone too far back. I wouldn't have near enough time to cover my entire life. Speed it up, boy!

The Little League games. The baseball scout in the stands. The big contract. The day I hit my seventy-third home run.

"Omigod," I realized. "I've got Barry Bonds's life passing before my eyes. Man, nothing's going right for me today."

Clayton aimed his knife, ready to make the first incision. I got ready for the worst and then . . .

Zap!

Finally. The morph had come, and not a second too soon. I opened my eyes slowly and . . .

"What the heck's going on?" said Clayton. "And what am I doing in this pan?"

Clayton? In the pan?

Yes, Clayton and I had been switched.

"Thank you, thank you!" I shouted.

This was going to be fun. Finally the chance I had waited for all my (or Barry Bonds's) life. Right then I could have done away with Clayton for all time. I could have taken over Clayton's life. Beating up kids and . . . well, the possibilities were mind-boggling. I mean, you could write a book. If you don't, I will.

I looked down at the box turtle I had once been and in those beady little eyes, I saw Clayton Moore. An extremely confused Clayton Moore.

That's when it hit me. I was certainly not the monster

that Clayton was. How could I ever slice apart the poor, defenseless, very conscious, living creature? I could never do that. Could I? No, I was a merciful human being.

I'll chloroform 'im first, I thought. That way he won't feel a thing.

And they say compassion is dead.

"Geez, peas," cried Clayton. "I was only jesting with you, Winchell, my friend, my pal, my *compadre*. I promise, I'll never be malevolent, speak in Latin, nor ridicule you in terms incomprehensible to you."

"What's all that supposed to mean?" I asked.

I really wouldn't have harmed Clayton. I just wanted to make him a little nervous. Teach him a lesson. I put down the dissecting knife, picked up Clayton, and looked him straight in the eyes.

"Listen, my *compadre*, I would never hurt you or offend you the way you've offended me. That's just plain wrong."

Of course, by now, the entire class was staring at me.

"Clayton," said Mr. Pringle gently. "Would you like to see the nurse?"

"Why would I want to see her?" reasoned the Clayton-looking me. "I already know what she looks like, and she's way too close to Principal Gudenplenty's office."

"Come on, Winchell," sweet-talked box turtle Clayton. "You're much too smart to think I would have harmed man, beast, or box turtle in any way. It was merely a game. I just wanted to see if I could fool you, that's all. Hurt you? Why, that would be criminal. I cringe that you would think that of me."

Zap!

I was turtle. Clayton was Clayton. This zap-morph-thing was now becoming commonplace to me. Now I assumed that when it happened, it was happening for the best.

I was so happy that I didn't injure Clayton when I had the chance, because now I was sure that Clayton wouldn't—

"You have got to be kidding," said the now Clayton-Clayton. "Did you just get off the dumb boat? How completely gullible. You, my Minkoid, are just a wee bit too weird to remain . . . alive."

And with that Clayton pressed the knife against my—

Zap!

"YOW!" screamed Clayton.

"What the . . . ?" I said in unfinished question form.

Okay, here's where it gets complicated, as if it wasn't that way about a hundred pages ago. We had been switched again. It might have been Clayton's body that held the knife, but once again, it was me inside actually maneuvering the hand. I quickly pulled the knife back.

"What are you, some kind of sick nut?" cried the now-panned Clayton. "You could hurt someone."

"Hurt someone?" I shot back. "It was you who was going to murder me."

At that very moment, in this world of unbelievable happenings, the most unbelievable event of all took place. Clayton broke down in tears of uncontrollable sadness.

TWENTY-SEVEN
Boo-boo Kitty

Clayton Moore crying? I had never seen Clayton like this, but I had seen enough bad television to know that Clayton was having some kind of emotional breakthrough.

"Boo-boo Kitty! Boo-boo Kitty!" he cried out.

It was heart wrenching. I rubbed Clayton's shell, attempting to settle the suffering, sadistic bully.

"What about Boo-boo Kitty?" I asked.

Still bawling, hardly able to form the words, Clayton could barely whimper.

"I loved Boo-boo."

Wow. Just hearing Clayton say he actually loved anything

seemed absolutely ker-razy.

"I took her wherever I went. At night, when I was in bed and there were lots of scary sounds, it was Boo-boo Kitty who was there to comfort me. When I was lost, wandering about in some strange neighborhood, it was Boo-boo Kitty who led me home.

"Then came that horrible day when Hermie Callaboosta showed up."

Hermie Callaboosta was legendary. Having failed recess fourteen years in a row, he was the only nineteen-year-old in kindergarten. The years of disappointment had hardened Hermie, and he responded by taking it out on much younger kids. So mean was Hermie that sometimes he would sit directly in front of the shorter children so they wouldn't be able to see the board.

"Hermie ran over Boo-boo Kitty with his bike . . . on purpose. She was flatter than a pancake. A Boo-boo Kitty pancake." Clayton sobbed.

"Why didn't you just buy another kitty?" I asked.

Clayton ignored me and wiped away his tears the best he could, not yet accustomed to the difficult-to-maneuver stubby legs of Hannibal. With halting words and a lump in his throat the size of a decent-sized pig, he continued.

"Boo-boo Kitty was my friend, and losing her hurt bad. I promised myself I wouldn't let anything hurt me again. If anyone was gonna hurt, I was going to make sure that I was doing the hurting."

I rolled my eyes. Luckily they didn't roll far, so I was able to find them quickly and place them back in their sockets before they dried up.

Finally I understood. I realized something that was far more significant than anything that had happened to date. Clayton and I weren't all that different. Well, Clayton was now a box turtle and I was Clayton, but you get the idea.

How ironic that Clayton had lost his pet and now he had become mine.

Clayton continued. "But, you know, now that I'm this turtle lying in a pan ready to be dissected, I'm beginning to see things in a totally different light. Here you are, someone who could get back at me for all the horrible things I've done to you, and yet you don't."

"Yeah. I am a pretty neat guy for a Mink-a-dink, aren't I?"

"Oh, yeah. I'm really sorry about making fun of your name and all."

"Well, I'm not. See, whether I'm a Mink or a turtle or even some guy with a Boo-boo Kitty, I'm still just as special as anyone else. No better, no worse. And nothing you can say or do will ever make me feel different again."

Then Clayton threw in the clincher.

"I'm thinking seriously that being a bully isn't as great a deal as I thought, Winchell," said Clayton. "I mean, here you are, this good guy, and you're the one that's in control."

He called me *Winchell*. That was even more shocking than hearing someone say that I was in control of anything. And as if almost to prove the point . . .

Zap!

To absolutely no one's surprise, especially not to anyone reading this, I was the turtle in the pan. But this time there was something different. Something magical. For now, in place of the maniacal glare that Clayton normally wore was a smile that could light up a stadium. Albeit an extremely tiny stadium with large magnifying mirrors to highlight whatever minimal glow was radiating from Clayton's smile.

Clayton lifted me from the pan and, to everyone's amazement, he waltzed out of the room holding me high above his head. Suddenly the other students began to applaud. The applause soon grew into a cheer, and Mr. Pringle, recalling his cheerleading days at old Dissect U., high kicked and led the chant of "Clayton Is Waltzing Out with a Turtle Held over His Head!"

TWENTY-EIGHT

I'm Goin' Home, Boys!

Clayton danced out of the building, followed by the entire school. No students. Just the school, which had somehow lifted itself off its moorings and bounded after Clayton like an adoring puppy. Or maybe a Boo-boo Kitty.

I wasn't sure where this was all leading, but when I saw that Clayton was actually carrying me toward my house, I brightened up as only an eleven-year-old boy stuck inside a box turtle can.

Clayton carefully placed me on the doorstep, rang the bell, then hid quietly in the rosebushes, even tactfully muffling the screams of pain he felt from the roses' thorns that were sticking a good half inch into his butt.

My mom, fresh from using her picture of an oven to bake my favorite apple pie with chopped walnuts in it, answered the door. Because of the whole mom/son time-space continuum thing that is way too complicated to explain in one book (at least this one), my long journey seemed like only a couple of moments to my mom.

"What is it, Hannibal? Where's Winchell? He's going to miss his birthday party."

My birthday. I had forgotten all about it, though being the only guest at my own party, I figured I wouldn't be missing much.

"And how did you ring the bell, you scallywag?"

Of course, I couldn't answer because way back then, as you know, turtles couldn't talk to human mothers. Luckily, with the few short mime lessons I had learned one summer at that creepy Camp Poison Ivy, I was able to communicate, although my meaning was a bit garbled.

"Winchell smelled down and soaked his candle?" asked my confused mom.

As you know, turtles make poor mimes.

I tried once more. This time was much better.

"Winchell fell down and broke his ankle? Oh, my!"

My mom picked me up and raced to where I had mimed my body could be found. Luckily it was only about half a mile away.

127

When she arrived, she found me, the me with Hannibal inside, still down on that ledge. A little hungry and a little cold, but otherwise just fine.

Mom lowered the ten-foot collapsible ladder she always carried in her purse for such occasions and climbed down.

She picked up my boy body with such gusto that she lost her balance and knocked over the ladder, which fell into the valley thousands of feet below.

I looked down at the two of them and just shook my tiny little box turtle head.

"Hannibal, go get help," implored my mom.

Isn't this where we came in? I knew I wasn't going to start this story all over again. I think we all have better things to do.

Just then Clayton arrived.

"Hello, Clayton," greeted Mom. "How are you today?"

"Just grand, Mrs. Mink. Better than I've been in a long time. How are you?"

"Oh, you know. Stuck down here on a ledge with Winchell."

With a wink to me, Clayton bent over the cliff and reached down, attempting to pull both my boy body and my mom from the ledge. He had my mother by the wrist, and she had my boy body hanging onto her ankle. And it was just in time, for the ledge, which had endured the weight of my body for so much time, and now the additional weight of my mother, who had done more than her share of tasting her wonderful pie recipes, finally could take it no more. It fell thousands of feet to the valley below.

Now Mom and my eleven-year-old boy body were swinging in the heavy breeze and tight grip of our hero, Clayton. Unfortunately, while Clayton was strong, being pinned down in that pan when he was a turtle had left him with a bit of muscle strain. Try as he might, his grip on Mom's wrist was slipping. It seemed that all 129 pages to this point would be just so many words and sentences, experiences and lessons, down the drain (or valley), for nature in the form of gravity would end up the victor. With Clayton's hand now only gripping the single pinky finger on my mom's right hand, there seemed no hope for . . .

Zap!

And, ladies and gentlemen, this was the most glorious *Zap!* of all. I became Winchell. The Winchell who would make it home in time for his birthday. Body and soul Winchell. Me Winchell, now standing next to Clayton on the top of the cliff. My ankle hurt badly but, like, who cared?

Down below my mother, still hanging by a single pinky, had not me, but Hannibal, Hannibal the turtle, grasping her leg. If Hannibal had not been one of the top weightlifters at the recent Turtle Olympics, she surely would not have been able to hold on.

With the load lighter, Clayton's grip tightened. I joined in the rescue effort, grabbing onto my mom's arm. Together we pulled Mom and Hannibal to safety.

"Winchell," said the breathless Clayton. "I hope there's some way you can forgive me for all the wrong I have done you."

"I can."

"Um. Even if you knew that I was the one who pushed you off . . .

THE CLIFF ♫♩?"

I was more than a little taken aback by this news. No wonder it had felt as though someone had pushed me off THE CLIFF ♫♩. Someone had. How could anyone forgive a person who put him through what seemed like years and years (and pages) of adversity?

"Sure." I smiled. "I'll still forgive you. Hey, look over there!"

Clayton looked, then turned back to me.

"I don't see any . . . "

That was when I made a choice. A pretty good one, I thought.

I clobbered Clayton with what had to be the best punch I ever threw.

I mean, sure, I was a nice guy, but come on, I wasn't a saint. At least not for a couple hundred years (that is, if they lower saint standards a whole bunch).

As a colorful swelling was closing Clayton's right eye, he smiled. He knew he had it coming. I placed my arm on Clayton's shoulder.

"And I would hope that, while even on my best days I'm no Boo-boo Kitty, you would think of me as your friend."

Ah-h-h. Is that sweet or what? We both shook hands as hugging would have been a wee bit too chummy.

We traipsed off to my house. I figured that just having Clayton, Hannibal, Mom, and Dad at my party would be fine. It's the quality of your guests, not the quantity, that matters. That is, unless you're charging them to attend. Then who cares about the quality as long as they can pay the admission?

As we arrived at my house, I realized how different I felt from when I had left. I had made a pledge to *experience life* before my birthday, and I had. And I learned that (Famous Quote Warning) "Experience is not what happens to you; it is what you do with what happens to you."★

The best thing was that I knew there were so many more experiences awaiting me (at least there better be; I have a three-book deal).

★ I'D LIKE TO TAKE CREDIT FOR THAT ONE, BUT THAT HONOR MUST GO TO THE BRILLIANT ENGLISH NOVELIST AND ESSAYIST MR. ALDOUS HUXLEY.

TWENTY-NINE
Pah-ty!

I t was dark as we entered my house. I wasn't stupid. I knew what that meant. Dad was a lot like Mother Nature. He still hadn't paid the electric bill.

Just then, I guess, he forked over the payment, because the lights came on and you'll never guess what happened next. Oh, you did.

Then you know that the entire living room was filled with people—and a couple of turtles. Hannibal's crowd.

All my classmates, including Clayton's gang, were there. Clayton gave them a look that I think meant: Don't mess with Winchell. He's a good guy and this whole bully stuff just doesn't work.

No one could say as much with a look as Clayton could.

I still wondered who was that someone or something behind my wild ride.

Just then I caught the eye of Hannibal, who gave me a knowing wink. But she wasn't going to tell me what I wanted to know, telepathically or otherwise. I guess who or what was in charge didn't matter as much as the fact that I actually took the ride. Maybe I had to figure things out for myself. Maybe that's why she only gave me a wink. Then Hannibal gave me another wink, and another, and another. That's when I realized she wasn't trying to tell me anything, only that she had something in her eye.

I blew out the burning candles on my favorite apple pie with the walnuts and everyone sang "Happy Birthday." And you know what? It was.

THIRTY

Oh, Yeah, One More Thing

Almost forgot. Those of you who are expecting some sort of moral are probably asking right now if there's a lesson to this story. To tell you the truth, I'm not one for moralizing, which is what a moral does. But since you did stick around this long, I guess I owe it to you.

I think it's rather obvious, but here it is. All together now . . .

"DON'T GO NEAR THE CLIFF♪♪!"